OUT OF THE PAN, INTO THE FIRE

She bucked and heaved. She almost threw me off but I scrabbled for better balance and a better grip with my boots on either side of her wildly thrashing body.

"Murderer," she moaned.

I let her feel some more of my weight.

"Give it up, Paula. Give it up."

"I'll kill you." Her voice was muffled by grass and dirt. "I'll rip your throat out."

"You won't," I said. "I'll put some pressure on your neck and you'll pass out. Then I'll unwind your scarf and tie you up. Is that what you want?"

I felt the cold metal against the nape of my neck and simultaneously heard the man's voice. "It's not what *she* wants that matters, Hardy. It's what *I* want."

Also by Peter Corris

MATRIMONIAL CAUSES

BEWARE OF THE DOG

A CLIFF HARDY NOVEL

Peter Corris

A Dell Book

Published by
Dell Publishing
a division of
Bantam Doubleday Dell Publishing Group, Inc.
1540 Broadway
New York, New York 10036

First published in Australia and New Zealand in 1992 by Bantam

ISBN: 0-440-21753-9

Reprinted by arrangement with Transworld Publishers Pty Limited

Printed in the United States of America

Published simultaneously in Canada

January 1995

10 9 8 7 6 5 4 3 2 1

RAD

For
Professor F. C. "Fred" Hollows

Beware of the Dog

1

DAN SANDERSON CLEARED HIS THROAT. "LAdies and gentlemen," he said, "I'd like you to meet Mr. Cliff Hardy, who has been a private enquiry agent for—"

"Longer than some of you have been alive," I said.

It got a laugh, but it was true. Some of the bright young faces looking at me didn't have twenty years on them, and that was how long I'd been in the business. We were gathered in a room in the Petersham College of TAFE, where

I was doing a guest lecturer spot in the Commercial Agents and Private Enquiry Agents course. When I got my license, it was different. All you needed were some solid citizens to vouch for you and an insurance company to give you the appropriate cover. As a former army officer and investigator for an insurance company I had no trouble qualifying. Now you have to do a course in small business practice, legal principles, and other things. I'm not sure I could pass it. Dan showed me the textbooks—very thick and not at all racy. But I didn't have to pass it. Instead, I was on the instructing end.

I talked for about forty minutes, giving them the spiel Glen Withers and I had worked out. I told them about the unwritten rules of confidentiality, the necessity for good relations with the police force, the advisability of having a friend in a newspaper office, and various other shortcuts to success. I told jokes, like the one about the client who had failed his driver's license test ten times and was convinced there was a conspiracy against him. I'd taken him seriously for a time. Then I'd stuck some L plates on my car and had him take me for a drive. End of case. And I told them about some sad ones, like the man who was sure that he was the father of his younger brother.

"The main thing to remember," I said in the windup, "is that as a PEA you are at the end of a long line. People have been let down by the law, their families, their friends, and all the authorities listed in the phone book. Often you are a last resort. That's an opportunity to exploit them, a reason to dismiss them, or a challenge. The choice is up to you."

I got a hand. Then it was question time. Nothing very tough: Did I carry a gun? Sometimes. Did I ever break the law? Not if I could help it. How many men had I killed? Two, one in defense of someone else's life, one by accident.

"You should be asking me if I can name all fifty of the United States of America."

A blond woman spoke from the back of the room. "You mean the work is often boring and that you have to kill time."

"That's right," I said.

Many eyes turned toward her.

"And can you name all fifty?"

"Usually," I said.

Time was up, and the students trooped out of the room. Dan Sanderson, usually a restrained type, shook my hand. "That went great, Cliff. Will you do the other class?"

Glen Withers had jacked it all up. Senior Sergeant Glenys Withers, that is. She was taking a break from hands-on policing and teaching at the Sydney annex of the Goulburn Police Academy. She had a flat in Petersham and spent three or four nights a week there; the other nights, her visits to Goulburn and my work permitting, she was at my place in Glebe. We were being very cautious about the whole thing; I had yet to sleep at Glen's flat. She had met Dan in a coffee shop and they got talking about their different teaching jobs—he was a lecturer in the commerce department of the Petersham College—and Glen produced a real live private eye for his students.

I'd enjoyed the lecture. Who wouldn't? Applause, appreciative young faces. "Sure, Dan," I said.

"I could probably get you a few tutorials, too," he said. "Could be the beginning of a new career for you, Cliff. You're a natural."

I shook my head. "I don't think so. Once was fine, twice might not be so good, and after that . . ."

"Well, see how it goes. Gotta rush. Thanks, Cliff. Give my best to Glen. The check'll be in the mail."

"Better be," I growled. He laughed and hurried out of the room. I gathered up the cards I'd scrawled a few notes on and followed him. The college is a grim redbrick structure that looks forbidding from the street, but the library, administrative offices, and classrooms are arranged in a three-story semicircle around a small garden, making it all surprisingly bright inside. I walked down the big-windowed corridors, enjoying the atmosphere. It had been a long time since my own—brief—university days, and things seemed to have changed enormously. There was an air of informality that had been totally lacking in my time, when we wore jackets and ties and tried to look older than we were. The students here were all ages and didn't care how they looked.

"Mr. Hardy. Could I speak to you?"

The woman who'd twigged about the boredom component of the job was standing under an archway at the top of the steps that led down to Crystal Street. I judged her age as late twenties; she was tall and slim with a pile of blond hair held back by a couple of combs and a velvet band. Her clothes were studentish: loose top, long skirt, boots. Her eyes were an alarmingly penetrating blue; they seemed to go right through me, out across the street, over the used-car yard opposite, and up beyond the rooftops.

I stuffed the cards into the pocket of my leather jacket and took the hand she held out. Smart move, to stick out your hand when you want to talk to someone. Takes a double-barreled rudeness to snub you. "Of course," I said. "Ms. . . . ?"

She laughed. "Mrs. I'm old-fashioned. Mrs. Paula Wilberforce. Paula."

She wasn't as sure of herself as she wanted to be. Her hand was smooth and warm. She looked the type to trick herself out with earrings and bangles, but the only jewelry she wore was a wedding ring.

"Hello, Paula. What can I do for you?"

"Are you going to be doing any more teaching in that course?"

"I don't think so. It was just a one-off for me. Something I haven't done before. I'll do a repeat performance for the other class, but that'll be it."

Her nicely shaped face fell into lines of disappointment. "Oh, I'm sorry."

"Come on. At a guess you were the smartest one there. You're not going to have any trouble getting your ticket." I glanced down at the backpack she had on the ground between her boots. It was stuffed with books and folders. "You're obviously a worker."

"I am," she said fiercely. "That's the trouble. I only enrolled in this course as backup to my Ph.D."

I must have started to edge away at that point. There's something about the intensity of people who want to be doctors of philosophy that disturbs me. "Well, I'm sorry I can't help you."

She grabbed five fingers' worth of leather sleeve. "You can! You can. You see, I'm doing my thesis on the role of the private enquiry agent in the legal system, and I'm having terrible trouble gathering material."

"I'm not surprised," I said. "We don't exactly go around shouting about our place in the scheme of things."

"No, but when I heard you talk today, I thought I might actually get something useful out of this course. You've had the experience."

"That's true," I said. "But—"

"Will you at least give me an interview? A long, in-depth session to let me get a handle on how experience feeds into the philosophical—"

That was enough for me. I pulled free of her and headed down the steps. "Afraid not, Mrs. Wilberforce. Professional code's against it. Sorry. Best of luck with your studies."

I could feel those blue eyes boring into my

spine as I walked along Crystal Street. There was something scary about her. I'd parked my car in a side street, and I actually checked to make sure she hadn't followed me before I drove off.

The thing is, business is slow. There's plenty of work around at the nastier end—industrial espionage, bugging, various forms of intimidation —but the bread-and-butter work of summons serving, bodyguarding, and money moving has shrunk. This is one of the reasons Glen encouraged me to take on the lecturing. We were sitting in the backyard at Glebe, catching a few faint rays of June afternoon sun. For no good reason, I was having my third glass of wine after lunch.

"You're underworked," Glen said.

"Is there such a thing?"

"Not for some people, but there is for you. You've got a low boredom threshold."

"Are you teaching community policing to the boys and girls in blue or psychology?"

"Don't be snaky, Cliff. Your mortgage on this place must be down to nothing by now. Business is bad. You need something else to occupy your time and energies. I'm only trying to help."

I put my arm around her as we leaned against the fibro wall of the outside laundry and bathroom. "I know you are, love. And you're right.

No kids, credit cards under control, and I own the car, such as it is. There is a bit of mortgage left, though. I had to buy Cyn out, remember, and she hiked up the price."

"The dreaded Cyn," Glen murmured. "I wonder if I'll ever get to meet her."

"Don't see why. I haven't met her for over ten years."

There wasn't much to say to that, but when Glen proposed that I talk to Dan Sanderson about lecturing to his students, I couldn't think of any way to refuse. Glen had a knack of being right in advance of my finding she was right. I was getting used to it.

As I drove to Darlinghurst, I was thinking that she'd been right again; after all, I'd enjoyed the time with the students and had been offered another spot. I could have scooted around the streets to Glen's flat and waited for her, but we had our rules. That night we were meeting for a meal in Glebe before going to my place, and such arrangements were sacrosanct. I hadn't been into the office for two days, and there was always a chance that someone had slipped a note under the door asking for my help in finding Lasseter's lost reef. I parked beside the church wall in St. Peters Lane and entered the building for what must have been the three thousandth time. *Stop it,* I thought. *You'll be counting the number of stairs you've climbed next, multiplying fifty-eight by three thousand. You're doing it already. Knock it off!*

There was nothing interesting under the door, where one of the other tenants, an iridologist, shoves my mail. That could mean a lot of things. The iridologist might be sick, or she might be pissed off with me for not availing myself of her services, or there just might not be anything interesting coming my way. The thought depressed me, and I sat at my desk watching the sun go down at around four-thirty. It was the shortest day of the year, still three hours to seeing Glen and dinnertime. There was only one thing to do.

I'd had one glass of red from the office cask and was thinking about a second when the phone rang. I grabbed it with relief.

"Hardy Investigations. Cliff Hardy speaking."

"I thought you might be there. You have a lonely look."

A woman's voice. Familiar. Who?

"Are you sure you've got the right number?"

"I'm sure, Mr. Hardy. This is Paula Wilberforce. I looked you up in the book. I'm sorry if I alarmed you this afternoon."

"You didn't alarm me, Mrs. Wilberforce."

"I think I did. Anyway, I wanted to apologize and to make it clear that nothing you tell me would ever be attributed to you in print. I'm simply asking for help, Mr. Hardy. Like one of your clients about whom you spoke so eloquently today."

Put it down to the early sunset or the wine or the total absence of anything interesting to do beyond the few routine jobs I had on hand—the upshot was that I agreed to allow Paula Wilberforce to interview me in my office the following day at 11:00 A.M. She sounded pathetically grateful, but I could see her blue eyes glittering. The woman was dangerous, even over the phone. I was thinking better of it as soon as I replaced the receiver, but what could I do? The snaky side of me said that it was Glen's fault for getting me into the academic racket in the first place. It would give us something interesting to talk about over dinner. I drew off another glass and stared through the window at the lights of the city. The angry traffic noises and the static of men and machines in conflict drifted up to me. Suddenly I wanted to be up at Whitebridge, at Glen's cottage overlooking the ocean with the lights of Newcastle away to the north and the sound of the waves on the beach. And I couldn't just up stakes and go because I had Mrs. Wilberforce to see tomorrow and Dan Sanderson's second class to talk to the day after that. *To hell with it*, I thought. *Maybe I should do a Ph.D.—Dr. Cliff Hardy, Senior Lecturer in Detection and Personal Mismanagement.* . . .

The knock at my door was sharp—anxious or angry. I called out, "Come in," and stuck the glass in the top drawer. A woman entered from the gloom of the passageway. She was smartly dressed in a navy suit with a red blouse. As I eased up politely from my chair, I saw that she was wearing nylon stockings and sneakers. She saw me looking and smiled. "I'll explain," she said. "You're Mr. Hardy."

I nodded. "Cliff Hardy. Please sit down. Your name is . . . ?"

"Verity Lamberte. You'd better write it down. The Lamberte has an *e* on the end."

I wrote the name on a pad and added "35, dark brown, shoulder length, wedding ring, 5ft. 7in." You never can tell with women; they can change their appearance in all sorts of cunning ways. Verity Lamberte was a vital, attractive sort of woman, a little too sharp-featured to be called good-looking, but with the confidence in her manners and gestures that good-looking women often have. She sat in my client chair, very composed and relaxed, with a big leather holdall on her lap. She unzipped the bag and held up a pair of expensive-looking high-heeled shoes. "I wear these to work and take them off the minute I can."

I nodded. "I would, too."

She smiled. "I was told you were a wit."

I was starting to like her and to wonder if she'd fancy a glass of cask red. "Who by?" I said.

"Barbara Winslow. The other reason I came in my runners is that I didn't like the look of this building of yours after dark. I've got some Mace in my bag, but I wouldn't like to have to deal with some lowlife while wearing high heels."

"I hope you locked your car."

"I did, and set the steering lock and the alarm."

"That should do it. You seem to be ready for anything, Mrs. Lamberte. Are you sure you need a private investigator?"

She put her hand into the bag and pulled out a package wrapped in brown paper. It was about the size of a thick paperback book, and it had been sealed with masking tape. The package had been opened, and the tape was now only partly holding the paper down. She slid it across the desk. "Have a look at this."

I released the tape where it was gripping and folded the paper back. Inside a lot of wadding consisting of strips torn from a newspaper were six pistol cartridges—.357 magnums, Winchester brand.

"That was posted to my husband," Verity Lamberte said. "I believe he is planning to kill me."

2

MRS. LAMBERTE TOLD ME THAT SHE AND HER husband, Patrick, were on the way to getting a divorce. The lawyers were working on a settlement.

"There's quite a lot of property involved and, unfortunately, custody questions. We have two children."

"How long were you married, Mrs. Lamberte?"

"Ten years, five good ones and five very bad. Michelle was born in the happy time; she's eight.

Shane is only four. We've been separated for six months. I'm claiming custody of both kids."

"You referred to your work. What do you do? And what does your husband do?"

"That's diplomatic. Not many men would put the questions that way around."

"I'm learning," I said.

"Patrick is . . . listen to me. I'm a partner in a small travel agency. I used to be an air hostess. We specialize in business travel. Patrick's an architect, and he has interests in other things."

"I gather the divorce isn't amicable?"

"Far from it. In the last few years before we separated we fought about everything."

"Such as?"

"Money, me working, the kids, drugs, lovers, real and imagined."

I leaned back in my chair. "That's a rich mixture. Perhaps you'd better tell me about this package, and we can work back from there."

"Right. Well, we . . . Patrick . . . God knows what you say under these circumstances. We have four acres in the Blue Mountains, at Mount Victoria. I heard that Patrick had been spending time up there, so I knew he must have built some kind of house. The land was worth about thirty thousand, and that's how it appeared in the preliminary settlement documents, so I went up there yesterday to check it out. Sure enough, he'd built a nice little timber and glass cabin looking out over the valley towards Bell's Road. D'you know the mountains, Mr. Hardy?"

"A bit. It sounds pretty good."

"It is. I'd say that property would be worth five times as much as Patrick has stated. That kind of fraud is typical of him."

"You searched the cabin and found the bullets?"

"No. God, no. I wouldn't do anything like that. I'm trying to play it very straight so as not to give him anything he can use to challenge the custody claim. That's why I'm here."

"Go on about the bullets."

"I went into the post office for some change to make a phone call. I'd only been up to Mount Victoria once or twice, and not for at least five or six years, but the woman in there recognized me and gave me the package. As you see, it's addressed to my husband."

A label on the package read: "Lamberte c/- PO Mt Vic 2765."

"Not exactly," I said.

She shrugged. "Well, I was never *there*, for God's sake. It had to be for him. I think that's

17

why she gave it to me—to be malicious. They must know what Patrick does up there."

"What would that be, do you think?"

"He's a very attractive man physically. He knows it and uses it."

I was beginning to get a picture of the Lambertes' marriage. The woman was telling her story well with a certain amount of conviction, but as with war, truth is the first victim of marital conflict. I had to feel for explanations other than the one Mrs. Lamberte had jumped to. "Perhaps your husband has taken up target shooting?"

She looked at me pityingly. "Mr. Hardy, he's threatened my life on more than one occasion."

"In front of witnesses?"

"Yes."

"Why don't you go to the police?"

"For the same reason I didn't break into his bloody love nest. Patrick's the professional. He can afford to hire the high-power legal help. I'm working on a shoestring, relatively speaking. If I . . . overstep my rights, invade his property, level false charges, Patrick will try to show that I'm unstable, an unfit mother. I can't take that risk. The only chance I have to get custody and a fair division of the property is to play strictly by the rules. But I'm afraid."

I studied her closely. Every hair remained in place, but there was an intensity and force in her voice that might have been her way of showing fear. It's one of the tricky aspects of the job—something I didn't tell the students about—judging whether a person you've met for the very first time is telling you the truth. "People say things they don't mean," I said. "I do, you do, everyone does. What makes you think your husband means what he's said?"

"Look, Mr. Hardy, I don't want to sound un-feeling, but Patrick Lamberte is a shit. He was a spoiled brat, an indulged adolescent, and a boy wonder. He had it very, very easy. He bowled me right over, I admit it. He propositioned me on a flight to London, and we were screwing in the Dorchester a few hours later. He established his architecture firm when there was tons of work around and money to burn. The recession has hit him really hard. He's got problems every way he turns. All I want to do is make sure that my future and that of my kids don't go down the drain when he does."

"I get the idea," I said. "If you take half of the assets now, he's finished."

"Possibly. It's a very delicate business. If there was any scandal now, the creditors could close in.

Everything could be lost. If it's all done quietly, there's a chance Patrick could restructure. I'm afraid he doesn't see it that way, though. He's irrational."

"You mentioned drugs."

"Patrick uses cocaine. It's one of the things that brought him unstuck."

"I'd have thought you could make some mileage out of that in the custody matter."

"I don't want to. If that came out, the whole financial house of cards could come down. You can see how tricky it all is. Barbara said you were a discreet and intelligent man."

Discreet and intelligent, I thought. *Wait till they hear I'm a tertiary teacher.* I'd helped Barbara Winslow unravel a difficult relationship with her politician husband. I suppose you could say I was discreet. I'd also been well paid. "What do you have in mind for me to do, Mrs. Lamberte?"

"Watch my husband. See if he meets with shady characters or seems to be plotting something. He's due to go up to Mount Victoria in four days. You could keep an eye on him. See if he tries to collect the package and how he reacts when it's not there."

I was intrigued, and I had another idea about what to do with the package, which only goes to show how intelligent I am. I told Mrs. Lamberte that I'd accept her case and charge her five hundred dollars as a retainer. She wrote out a check without blinking. I got her address and that of her husband and the name of the lawyer who was acting for her. That about concluded our business. I gave her a receipt, locked the package and her money in a drawer of my desk, and offered to escort her to her car. She refused, and I was relieved. Gave me a chance to finish my drink.

"So, how did it go?" Glen said.

We were sitting in a Thai restaurant on Glebe Point Road. I don't care for Thai food much, but Glen does and we went Italian the last time we ate out. I was thinking about the Lamberte bullets. "How did what go?"

"The talk at the college, what d'you think?"

"Oh, it was fun. I enjoyed it. Dan was happy."

"I thought you were going to be nervous."

"I was okay as soon as I got my first laugh."

"How soon was that?"

"Right off."

I told Glen how the lecture had gone while we waited for our food. She rubbed the arm she'd taken a bullet in the previous year. That was in Newcastle soon after we met. The wound was one of the reasons she'd swapped policing for teaching. Rubbing it had become a habit. Sometimes I rubbed it for her in bed, along with other parts. We enjoyed touching and talking, and what else is there, really? She spent part of her time at the academy and part in police stations and offices showing the trainees the ropes. She liked it and didn't seem to miss the operational work. She kept very fit in a gym and drank more mineral water than wine. I drank more wine than mineral water but less than I used to, and the long weekend walks we took kept me reasonably springy.

I ate a forkful of spiced beef. "Dan wants me to give the talk again. He said he could probably get me steady work."

Glen lifted one of her dark eyebrows. "Interested?"

"Shit, no. I think the novelty'd soon wear off. Then this crazy woman came up to me . . ."

"Hmm, is she what you were thinking about so intently you ordered spiced beef, which you don't like?"

"No. Something else."

I told her about Paula Wilberforce and her Ph.D., making light of it.

"Watch her," Glen said. "The teacher-student relationship is sexual dynamite."

"Know all about it, do you, love?"

"You bet. I could be having it off with two of the smartest, fittest nineteen-year-olds in Sydney. They're both mad about me."

"Well?"

"Smart and fit isn't everything. What about you? Are you attracted?"

"Blue eyes aren't everything."

"What?"

"She's got these intensely blue eyes. Make her look a bit mad. She might be, in fact. I wish I hadn't agreed to see her tomorrow. I've got something much more interesting on."

"Are you going to tell me about it?"

"If it develops. How about swapping me some chicken with nuts for some spiced beef?"

3

AT NINE FORTY-FIVE THE NEXT MORNING I
was sitting at my desk with a stick-on label,
ballpoint pen, and masking tape, rewrapping and
readdressing the Lamberte ammunition package.
An hour before, I'd taken the bullets to a gun-
freak friend who loads his own ammunition.
He'd obliged me by removing the gunpowder
from the .357s.

"Still dangerous, Cliff," he'd said. "Still got a
capacity to go off pop."

I'm no expert forger, but the block capitals on

25

the original label weren't difficult to copy, and there were no eccentric spellings or European sevens to worry about. I'd almost finished the job to my satisfaction when Paula Wilberforce walked in without knocking.

"Hi. What's that?"

I turned the package over so that the label faced down and folded up the original wrapping. "You're early," I said.

She dropped her backpack to the floor and sat down. "I like to be early. Catch people napping. Though you seem to have been working very seriously. What *is* that? It looks like a book. What's the title?"

"*Etiquette*, by Emily Post."

She jumped up, turned, and left the room, closing the door behind her. Then she knocked and opened the door an inch. "Better?"

I said, "Come in, Mrs. Wilberforce."

She strode back to the chair. She was wearing the same clothes she'd had on yesterday, and her eyes were the same glittering blue. "I'm pushy," she said. "I know it. It puts some people off. I hope you won't be one of them."

"I can be pushy myself. Let's move this along, Mrs. Wilberforce. Have you got a questionnaire or something? I'm rather busy today."

"You're not busy. You're sitting here wrapping up a book. There're no files in evidence. There's dust on the furniture and"—she leaned forward—"wine stains on the desk. How's the private detective business?"

"Lousy. Aren't you going to tape this?"

"I never tape the preliminary session."

"There is going to be only one session, Mrs. Wilberforce. Busy or not, I don't want to talk about what I do. I agreed to see you in a moment of weakness. I was flattered by the attention I got yesterday from you and your classmates."

"They're not my classmates!" she flared. "I'm in an advanced sociology seminar at UTS."

"Good for you. But I really don't think I can help you."

"You can, but you won't. Okay, that's fine. I can make something of that." She reached into the backpack and took out a miniature tape recorder. "We'll do it your way. How long have you been a PEA?"

"I told you that yesterday. A long time."

"Good crack, as I recall. But I mean precisely."

"Mrs. Wilberforce, I—"

She clicked off the recorder. "Okay. Let me spend a day with you. See what your day is like."

"No."

Tears appearing in the blue eyes seemed to enlarge them and make them not blurry but even more penetrating. "Please," she said. Her wide, handsome mouth parted, revealing strong white teeth. A vein throbbed in the smooth tan column of her neck.

"Absolutely not."

"Why not?"

"You guessed right. I'm not actually doing much today. I've got a man to see in Granville, later." I tapped the package. "This has to do with a case, but it doesn't require any significant action today." *Bugger it*, I thought. *Why did I tell her that?*

She blinked and wiped the tears away with the back of her hand. "Okay," she said. She turned the recorder on again and proceeded to interview me politely and intelligently for about twenty minutes, asking sensible, not overly intrusive questions and making perceptive responses.

"Thank you for your time, Mr. Hardy." She spoke without irony or sarcasm. She checked that the recorder had functioned properly, put it away in her bag, and stood up. I stood, too, and took the hand she extended.

I mumbled something about being glad to help.

"Are you going to talk to Mr. Sanderson's other class?"

"I guess so. Why?"

"No reason. Thanks again. Bye."

I watched her walk to the door. Her thick blond hair hung halfway down her back, and her movements were graceful. She closed the door and opened it again almost immediately. I caught a flash of her eyes. "See you again," she said.

The box of bullets had been sent from the post office on Broadway near the brewery that used to have a big Tooth's sign over the gateway. Now the sign says Carlton. I preferred the old sign and the old beer. I parked in Rose Street and walked to the post office. I might have been wasting my time. It might not matter to the recipient where the package was posted from, but then again, it might. It was against the law to put live ammunition, even doctored like this lot, through the post, but like the original sender, I hadn't included a return address, so who would ever know? I dispatched the parcel and got a receipt for the postage—an item for Mrs. Lamberte's account.

"How long will that take, would you say?"

The pimply-faced youth behind the counter looked at the address. "Two days, three at the outside."

"Guaranteed?"

"You can priority pay it if you want."

A priority sticker would give the parcel a very different appearance. I shook my head and left the post office.

That left me with the Granville job. Nothing much to it. Cy Sackville wanted a certain Lionel Peckham to appear as a material witness in a case involving one of his valued clients. Cy had worked out an immunity deal with the prosecution for Peckham, but he couldn't locate him to inform him of the fact. Cy had explained the complicated legal maneuvers involved but had lost me in the telling. All that mattered to me was that I was obligated to him for many legal services beyond the bounds of duty and often unpaid for. I had traced Peckham to a junkyard in Granville. All I had to do was confront him, show him the letter that guaranteed him immunity, and tell him where and when to show up. Easy.

As I cruised past the junkyard, I saw at once that it was not going to be so easy. The place was in a cul-de-sac near the railway line and well away from houses and activities carried on by honest citizens. The weed-choked, rusted cyclone fence, the galvanized iron shed set well back from the street, and the rusting Ford, Holden, and Toyota bodies screamed hot cars, hot parts, hot whatever-you-cared-to-name. That was a worry. More of a worry was the dog.

An Alsatian. Black and a dirty yellow. Very mean. It was chained up near the gate to the lot so that it couldn't quite get out to the pavement. It looked as if it wanted to more than it wanted its next meal, and the ribs showing through its scruffy hide suggested meals weren't all that frequent. As cars drove past, it strained at the chain. A man walked by on the other side of the street, and the dog stretched the chain to its last link as it watched him out of sight.

I parked opposite the gate about thirty yards from the dog. It watched me, and I watched it. I also looked into the yard for signs of human life. A big man wearing overalls wandered into view carrying what looked like a gearbox. He answered the description Cy had given me: six feet two, 220 pounds, fortyish, ginger hair. I got out of the car and crossed the road. The dog started to bark when I was still twenty yards away, and it kept on barking until I stood just outside the length of the chain. The man in the overalls looked toward the gate. He put the piece of machinery down and wiped his hands on a rag.

I took out Cy's letter in its pure white envelope and waved it like a flag of truce. "Mr. Peckham," I yelled. "Good news."

The dog barked louder.

"Call him off. I want to talk to you."

He shook his head. I wondered whether I could hurdle the dog and get beyond the reach of the chain before it recovered. Glen might have made it; I knew I had no chance. I went back to the car and took my .38 Smith & Wesson from the glove box. Back across the street I held the pistol at arm's length. The dog was rearing up, pressing forward. If a link in the chain or the fastening to its collar gave, blood would have to flow. I lifted the gun, then brought it down slowly and pointed it at the dog's head.

"Don't!"

He hurried forward, making soothing noises to the dog, which responded immediately, dropping to its haunches and assuming a sort of His Master's Voice position. It stayed there, growling quietly, as he stroked its ears and rubbed the thick fur around its collar. I put the gun in the pocket of my jacket.

"What d'you fuckin' want?"

"Mr. Peckham?"

"If I am?"

"If you are, you've got immunity in the Williamson matter. Signed and sealed."

"Says who?"

"I've got the papers."

"You've also got a fuckin' gun."

"I'll put it back in the car if you like. Just read this."

He held out his hand. The dog growled. I tossed the envelope to him. He caught it. The dog looked at me as if I'd denied it a bone. Peckham opened the envelope and scanned the several sheets of paper inside.

"Looks okay," he grunted.

"It's the best offer you're going to get. Phone Sackville now. He'll see you right."

He nodded and stuffed the papers into the front pocket of his overall. "Would you have shot the dog?"

"Maybe," I said. "What's its name?"

"Fenech."

Peckham gave the dog's fur a last scratch and

turned his back on both of us. I drove to the nearest shopping center and bought the biggest tin of dog food I could find. Back outside the junkyard, I opened the tin with my Swiss army knife and used the blade to loosen the contents. Fenech was rampant again. I stood at a safe distance and shot the contents of the tin in its direction. The mess of meat and gristle and cereal hit the ground and Fenech buried his muzzle in it as if he were trying to burrow through it to China.

I drove back to the city feeling that I'd handled the situation reasonably well. Crude but effective. Hire Hardy for results. It was a nonpaying job. I owed Cy Sackville more money than I'd ever be able to pay off, but there was some satisfaction in reducing the debt fractionally. As I drove, I thought about the Lamberte matter. There were a few questions: How did Verity Lamberte come to know so much about her estranged husband's movements? What other slants were there on the damaged marriage? What exactly had she meant by "lovers, real and imagined"? How serious was Patrick Lamberte's drug problem? Did it put him in touch with suppliers of arms and ammunition?

I was still mulling these questions over when I pulled up outside my house in Glebe, the one with the small mortgage and big need for renovations. I hadn't eaten since the rushed toast and coffee breakfast I'd shared with Glen that morning. She'd driven to Goulburn, had probably had lunch, and here I was at 2:30 P.M. with a rumbling stomach. I was stiff, too, from the driving. I pushed open the gate and brushed past the overgrown creeper that veils the front porch. I had my key out and was squinting in the gloom at the lock.

"Stand right there."

I whipped my head to the right. Paula Wilberforce stood on the porch near the party wall three yards away. She had both hands raised and extended straight out in front of her. What she was holding looked like a gun.

"How do you think the dog felt?"

I wasn't in the mood. Anger rose in me, and I felt an adrenaline rush, banishing stiffness and hunger. I sidestepped and rushed her, bent low. I chopped up at her wrists and hacked at her ankles with a short kick. She screeched, dropped the gun, and almost collapsed. She hopped to take the pressure off her left leg where my kick had caught her. I bent down and picked up the object she'd dropped. It was a toy gun, plastic, light as a feather. Not even a water pistol.

"What the hell are you playing at?"

"I wanted you to feel what the dog felt."

"You're mad."

"What the man felt, then."

"You followed me all the way out there?"

"Sure. I told you I wanted to know how you operate. Now I think I understand."

I could have told her that I'd gone back and made my peace with the dog, but I was too angry. "I doubt it. You need help."

"Help me then."

"You know what I mean."

"Who was that man? What was in the envelope?"

I tossed the toy to her. She caught it deftly, still favoring one leg. "Go away, Mrs. Wilberforce."

"I followed you. I parked just a little way down the street. Shouldn't you have noticed me? Are you getting too old for what you do?"

I shoved the key in the lock. "Go away!"

Her voice changed, taking on the severe, serious tone she'd finally adopted in the interview. "Mr. Hardy. One more thing."

I had the door open. "What?"

"I can't help wondering what was in that parcel you posted. You seemed terribly concerned about it."

4

THE CAT WITH NO NAME GREETED ME AS I
came through the door. It followed me down the
hall into the kitchen and stood over me until I
opened a tin of food for it. The way I felt I'd
have opened two tins if it had insisted. I
searched my memory for some recollection of
Paula Wilberforce at the post office, on the road,
and at Granville—some subconscious mental image that I hadn't bothered to process. Nothing.
Her question hit the nail on the head. Here I
was, congratulating myself on handling a tricky

situation with aplomb, and I hadn't noticed a crazy woman keeping tabs on me in broad daylight.

The implications of that failure troubled me more than the fact of her attentions. I'd dealt with unstable women before—telephone callers, letter writers, window breakers. They tend to have low stamina and to be pretty easily deflected on to some other grievance. *Are you getting too old for this? Maybe you should take Dan Sanderson up on his offer.* I shook the thought off as I made myself a sandwich and poured a big glass of white wine. It wasn't even an option. I was of value as an instructor *because* I was a practitioner. Maybe it was a blessing in disguise, a reminder not to get slack just because most of the things I do I've done a thousand times before.

I ate the food and drank the wine. I had the shower I'd missed in the morning; then I set about tidying the kitchen Glen and I had left in such a hurry. I went upstairs to do the same in the bedroom. The bed was a mess with the fitted bottom sheet adrift and the blankets in a tangle. Our lovemaking after last night's meal had been vigorous, and both of us were restless sleepers, contending for space and the bedclothes. I sat down on Glen's side. I could smell her in the sheets and on the pillows. I wouldn't have her tonight to talk to or to hold. I missed her. *Soft, Hardy. You're getting soft.* I straightened the bed roughly, collected the glasses and mugs, and went down to make more mess in the kitchen.

Dan Sanderson answered his phone on the first ring, he was that kind of man.

"Dan?" I said. "This is Hardy."

"You're not crying off? It's ten tomorrow. That leaves you all day to fight crime."

"No. I'll be there. I just wanted some information about one of your students—Mrs. Paula Wilberforce."

"Hey, I thought you were happily attached."

"I am. This woman's harassing me. I can handle it, don't worry. I just thought a little extra dope might help."

"Just a sec. I'll get her on screen."

I heard the tapping of keys and wondered whether I should computerize my operation. Maybe the computer would analyze all my cases and come up with solutions in advance. Then it wouldn't matter that a madwoman could follow me around and stick me up on my own front porch.

"Got her," Dan said. "Bright, very bright. HDs all the way in her B.A. Doing a Ph.D. on wards of the state and recidivism."

"What?"

"You know, broken homes and criminal careers. Roger Maurice is her supervisor. I know him slightly."

"Married, right?"

"Not according to what I have here. Look, Cliff, I shouldn't really be doing this."

"Come on, we're almost colleagues and my girlfriend's a policeperson. Just give me her address and phone number, and that'll be it. It's no big deal, really."

He gave me the address, in Lindfield. As an afterthought I got the contact number for Dr. Roger Maurice at UTS. Then I made a few calls. Paula Wilberforce was the registered owner of a white Honda Civic, KTP 232. Her credit rating was shaky. She was over her limit on Bankcard and teetering on the brink of having her Visa card snipped in half. Her last tax assessment on an income of over eighty thousand dollars hadn't been paid, and her telephone and electricity accounts were in arrears. While I was at it, I ran checks on Patrick and Verity Lamberte. An Escort for her, a Saab for him. She was sitting pat; he was seriously overextended.

I needed sausages, bread, and beer for the evening meal I was planning. I went out to the street and stopped to check the mailbox, which I'd neglected to do on the way in. I glanced at my car; the light seemed to be hitting the windshield oddly. Then I saw that it was shattered, with only cloudy segments of glass clinging around the frame. I swore. The passenger side window in the front was broken as well, and the glove box was hanging open. The plastic gun was sitting on the front seat. I felt my stomach lurch as I reached through to feel inside the glove compartment. The .38 wasn't there. I leaned back against the car with my head throbbing. *Criminal neglect to leave the gun inside the car, especially after you knew she'd seen your every move. And what to do about it?*

The right thing to do was to notify the police, but I didn't think I could face the humiliation and the complications. I could see the grins on the faces of the cops in the Glebe station. Then would come the serious stuff—the warnings, the threats to lift my license. It *was* serious—an unstable woman running loose with a loaded pistol. It might even get into the press. I groaned aloud at that thought and gave up the idea of telling the police, at least for now. Then another thought struck me. She'd pointed a toy gun at me; would she do the same with a real one? I went back inside and phoned one of the places that will send out a mobile van to replace your windshield. I gave them the specifications of the windshield and window, accepted their quote, and told them where I'd leave the check. They promised to do it "today." Then I called a cab.

I was poor company for the cabbie on the drive to Lindfield. He made the correct assumption that I was a Balmain supporter and commiserated with me about the side's performance in the Winfield Cup. I barely listened, scarcely responded, even though I've started to take more interest in League lately as a result of Glen's being a passionate Newcastle supporter. It was after five and quite dark and cool by the time we got to Lindfield. There was a big fare on the meter that I wasn't going to be able to lay off on anyone as an expense, and I was in a foul temper. The taxi cruised along the wide, tree-lined street while I peered out, trying to spot numbers.

"Don't these people put numbers on their gateposts?" I grumbled.

"Don't ask me, mate. I live in St. Peters. We don't have bloody gateposts."

I laughed. "Yeah, right. Well, let's see if we can spot number twelve through all this greenery."

We found it. The house was a big, rambling timber job with a botanical garden in front and a wide wood-block driveway leading to a two-vehicle carport. It fitted right in with its neighbors to either side—solid four-hundred-thousand-dollar places with all the trimmings. The only difference was that number 12 was obviously empty. Local newspapers had accumulated by the gate, and a few telltale weeds sprouted through the woodblocks. Lights were showing in the other houses, but number 12 was dark. There was also a large For Sale sign mounted over the center of the front hedge. The agents were Climpson & Carter of Chatswood.

"Chatswood," I said to the driver. "Ten bucks in it for you if you make it before five-thirty."

He didn't. The real estate agent's office was closed up tight, and from long experience, I had no hopes of learning anything useful from trying the after-hours number.

By this time the driver and I were chatty. "Where to now, mate?" he said.

"Back to Glebe, thanks. We'll have to stop at an autobank on the way so's I can pay you."

"No worries. What d'you think of that Alan Jones?"

"I try not to think about him. Who d'you support?"

"Penrith, mate."

"I might have known."

The windshield repairers hadn't yet arrived when I got back to Glebe. I walked up Glebe Point Road and bought a hamburger and a six-pack of Toohey's Blue Label. The hamburger was tasteless, or maybe I was tasting only bile. I drank three cans of beer and rang Glen at the hotel where she usually stayed when she was overnight in Goulburn. She'd registered but wasn't in her room. I stood by the front window, looking out at the car. If it sat there all night, the radio'd be gone for sure in the morning. I guessed Paula Wilberforce had done her damage while I was under the shower.

I went out and retrieved the toy gun from the front seat. A crude model of a .357 magnum, it looked unreal, an obvious toy. But in the woman's fist, as she stood there with her legs braced and both hands up, TV style, it had looked very real. I tried to feel sorry for her, but I couldn't. If my gun was used in a crime, I was in real trouble. I had to find her and it, fast. I ground my teeth and glared at my neighbors' cars with their intact windows and windshield. Still no sign of the men with the glass.

I went inside and tried the number for Dr. Roger Maurice. It was engaged, and I swore. I sat with the phone in my hand, punching the redial button until I got an answer.

"Dr. Maurice, my name's Cliff Hardy. I—"

"Dan Sanderson phoned me, Mr. Hardy. I gather you're having trouble with Paula Wilber-force."

"You could say that. What can you tell me about her? I gather she's a Ph.D. student."

"She was. Dropped out a month or so ago."

"What was her research topic?"

"She was supposed to be writing a study of women's refuges. I never saw any signs that she was serious about it. Tell me, has she . . . done any damage?"

"Yes. Is she sane, do you think?"

"Far from it. She broke into my room at the university and wrecked it. This was after I pointed out that she hadn't begun to fulfill the requirements of her course. She's wealthy, did you know?"

"Not exactly. I went to her place in Lindfield, but it's up for sale. Big house."

"She inherited a lot of money. She's very dangerous, Mr. Hardy. She harassed me for months. I got her to see a student counselor, and his report was, well . . . disturbing. If she's transferred her attentions to you, you've got a real problem."

"Does she have a doctor?"

"Now that you mention it, yes. I've got some of this stuff on disc. I could look it up and give you a ring back in a few minutes if you'd like."

I thanked him and gave him my number. Another computer man. Gave him an edge. What I didn't remember I didn't know. I looked out the window again. Nothing. At least it wasn't raining. I had another can of beer.

"Dr. John Holmes," Maurice said when he rang back. "Psychiatrist."

"Woollahra. I know him. Many thanks."

He wished me the best of luck, with feeling. I'd met Dr. Holmes a few years back, when I was trying to find a freaked-out writer bent on destroying himself and a few others. I found him, but too late, and Dr. Holmes wasn't a hell of a big help. Still, it was something to cling to.

Maybe Paula Wilberforce went to see him every week and would be happy to put my gun on his big, polished desk. I went to the cupboard under the stairs where I keep another gun—an unlicensed Colt .45 automatic. It was an early model that didn't have the extra safety grip that has to be squeezed before the weapon can operate. I've never liked it, always thought of it as a dangerous piece of equipment, but I keep it oiled and clean. I worked the slide and ran a rag over it, then put it away in the dark cupboard.

A light flashed in the front window. Dial a Windshield had arrived. Normally I'd have gone out to watch them work and thanked them for their efforts, but the reverses of the day had soured me. I stood at the window and watched their efficient movements as they suctioned out the broken glass and fitted the new windshield and window. Two men performed the operation inside thirty minutes. They took the check, locked the doors, and went on their way. I envied them the simplicity and usefulness of their line of work.

It was close to eleven o'clock when I finally got through to Glen. She sounded tired and told me she'd had a hell of a day defending some of her liberal positions on firearms and the use of vehicles. "How was your day?" she said.

What could I say? I couldn't tell her about the plastic gun and the real one. She'd have reported the theft immediately, whatever I said. I told her the day had been dull apart from a broken windshield.

"Shit. Were you hurt?"

"No, no. Cost a couple of hundred bucks, though."

"Look, Cliff, I'm going to have to stay another night. There's a new intake I have to talk to and some other things to do."

"Okay, but I won't be here the day after. I've got to go up to the Blue Mountains."

"For how long?"

"I don't know."

It was one of those difficult moments we encountered from time to time. She didn't expect me to tell her what I was doing. I wanted to, but we both knew it wouldn't work. It was an uncomfortable thing, especially over the phone.

"So," I said. "Take care of yourself."

"You too. I'm in bed. I wish you were here."

"Me too. What're you wearing?"

"It's bloody freezing. I've got my tracka on."

Glen had made a trip to New Caledonia as part

of her recovery from her wound and returned with some pleasing French sleepwear. It amused her to see its effect on me. It amused us both. "Good," I said.

5

I MADE A MESS OF THE LECTURE. I WAS NER-
vous and distracted. I couldn't remember much
of what I'd said the first time and kept getting
my sentences tangled up. I was on the lookout
for Paula Wilberforce and didn't relax for the
whole time. I was impatient with the question-
ers. Altogether an unimpressive performance. No
applause. When, to everyone's relief, it was over,
I apologized to Sanderson.

"That's okay," he said. "Happens. Is it to do
with Ms. Wilberforce?"

"Yeah. I really need to get in touch with her. That Lindfield address you gave me's a frost. It's up for sale, and the agents won't tell me a thing about her."

I'd telephoned Climpson & Carter at five minutes past nine and drawn a complete blank. I asked Sanderson if he knew anything at all about the woman that might help me. I told him that Dr. Maurice had been helpful up to a point, and this seemed to encourage him. He said he might have something and went to his office, which was a small, narrow, cell-like room with a window looking out over Crystal Street. The window was too dirty to look through, but Crystal Street isn't much to see. Dan opened drawers in a filing cabinet and banged them shut. Then he opened the same drawers again. It seemed to be his way of finding things.

"Thought so." He held up a card. "She was sick and got me to post her essay back. I remember that it was a different address from the one on her enrollment. Cliff, I'm not sure I should be doing this."

I pulled out the receipt the windshield boys had left in the car. "Take a look at this. Your bloody student trashed my car yesterday. She followed me on a job. She's making a bloody nuisance of herself, and I have to put a stop to it."

Dan handed the note over. It was a few scrawled lines asking him to post her essay to 74B St. Marks Road, Randwick.

"You did it? And she got it?"

"Yep. What're you going to do, Cliff?"

"Convince her of the error of her ways. Thanks a lot, Dan. Sorry again about the lousy performance."

He grunted, not happy.

The weather had improved, and my mood had lifted. At least I had some line to follow other than trying to get an appointment with Dr. Holmes. I knew from experience that that would be hard, and getting information from him even harder. It was warm in the car, so I wound the windows down. The new window fitted fine, and all seemed well with the windshield. A few minute particles of glass glittered along the top of the dashboard. Inevitably there would be other specks in the seats and on the floor, but the specialists had done a good job. As I drove to Randwick, the thought struck me that the well-heeled Ms. Wilberforce might be persuaded to pay for the damage. I was feeling better by the minute.

The house was a three-story sandstone mansion set in an elevated position on a big corner block. There was a high white wooden fence across the front and an even higher brick wall along the street side. The gate in the front fence had some sort of security lock. I wandered along the side to where the double garage stood open. A dusty dark blue Land Rover was parked in one of the spaces; the other was empty. Through an open door at the back of the garage I could see into number 74B's yard: swimming pool enclosed in some kind of solarium, clippered lawn, flower beds, native trees. The area appeared to trap all the available sun and light.

I walked through the garage into this patch of suburban paradise. Inside the solarium a man was lying on a cane lounge. He was old, wrinkled like a turtle, and brown as a much-oiled boot. He was also naked apart from sunglasses. His thin body was stretched out on the lounge like a lizard basking in the sun. A copy of the *Financial Review* was propped up in front of him, held by hands that trembled slightly as he turned the page. A bright red inflated raft drifted in the pool. I could hear music, very faintly, possibly coming from inside the house. The solarium was an aluminum frame fitted with a series of swivel-mounted plastic panels. I opened one of the panels and stepped inside. The temperature went up twenty degrees, and sweat broke out around my collar and started to run down my chest.

"Excuse me."

He slowly lowered the paper but did not place it across his genitals. No false modesty here. He slid the shades down to the end of his beaky nose. The face he turned toward me was a mask of urbanity: clipped white mustache, fringe of hair the same color around a bald mahogany skull, and piercingly blue eyes, undimmed by his considerable age.

"You are trespassing, sir."

"I'm here on business."

"Have you ever heard of Evelyn Waugh?"

"The novelist? Yes."

"I'm told that on the gate outside his house he had a sign reading, 'No admittance on business.' I've always admired Evelyn Waugh. I think you should leave."

I moved closer and looked at him. It was impossible to guess his age. He could have been a sun-ravaged sixty or a sun-preserved eighty. The smooth face and clear blue eyes suggested sixty; the wrinkled, reptilian penis and scrotum suggested the octogenarian.

I said, "Maybe Waugh's daughter or granddaughter didn't cause him a whole lot of trouble."

He removed the sunglasses and flipped them onto the grass beside his lounge. "Oh, God, not again."

"I'm afraid so, Mr. Wilberforce."

"Sir Phillip."

"I'm a republican. Sorry."

He laughed, revealing an almost full set of white, strong-looking teeth. "So was I as a young man. Well, what's Paula been up to? She's my daughter, by the way. I'm eighty. Her mother was half my age when Paula was born—twenty-five. I regard that as the proper ratio."

"You have to keep getting younger women to maintain it."

"Exactly. How much does Paula owe you?"

"It's not a matter of money. She has something of mine that I want returned."

"What?"

I was tired of standing to attention in front of this old stager. Near the end of the pool there was a cane chair over which a blue terry cloth bathrobe had been thrown. I moved across, slung the bathrobe onto the tiled edge of the pool, and brought the chair close to the lounge. I sat down, took out my PEA license, and showed it to Sir Phillip.

"Phil," I said, "your little Paula's been a very bad girl. She damaged my property and took something that belongs to me. I think she's a very sick woman, but if you're her father, that's your problem, not mine. All I want to do is get back what's mine and give her a warning."

He leaned forward to examine the license folder, then sank back on the lounge. For the first time he sounded old. "She's been receiving warnings for twenty-five years, Mr. Hardy. None have been heeded."

"Where is she?"

"She has a house in Lindfield. I bought it for her."

"I hope your name's on the title deeds. It's up for sale. She's not there."

Finally he let go of the newspaper. It flopped down to cover his genitals and skinny thighs. "God, not again."

"Meaning?"

"Paula attended eight primary and six secondary schools. She dropped out of university at least five times. She killed her mother."

"What?"

"Figuratively speaking. She lived for six months with some poor unfortunate who thought he could mean something to her. I doubt he's ever recovered from the experience. She is brilliant, seductive, a walking disaster. I hope you are not involved with her sexually. If you are, and she has dropped out of sight, I strongly advise you to leave well enough alone."

There was a lot in that to chew on, and I watched him closely as he spoke. He was evidently in the throes of powerful emotions, but it was impossible to tell in what directions they were pulling him.

"It's nothing like that. But it's very important that I see her. I take it she's not here?"

"No. Why is it so important?"

"I'd rather not say."

He nodded. He understood. I wondered what that understanding said about him and his relationship with his daughter. I looked up at the big house, which was starting to cast a shadow that would eventually fall across the solarium. It had a high-gabled slate roof and two attic rooms on the top level. A creeper covered most of the back wall.

"Yes, I live here alone, if that's what you're thinking. I've had three wives and I'm never quite sure how many children. A few of doubtful paternity and the wives brought others with them, you see. I couldn't get used to a small place, not at my age."

"Who drives the Land Rover?"

"I do. I drive it to places where there are no people. Then I go bush walking."

I believed him. He couldn't have weighed more than 135 pounds, and his thin legs looked strong. "Look," I said, "she followed me the other day. There's a chance she could be doing it again today. Could I go up to the top there and take a look around? I promise not to lift the family silver."

He sighed and picked up his paper. "Be my guest, but I must tell you that it's fruitless to anticipate what Paula will do. Whatever you think of she has most likely done the opposite."

I walked through the solarium and was grateful for the coolness of the air between it and the house. I stepped through a sliding door into a huge kitchen with a flagstone floor. The bottom story was given over to a living-cum-dining room,

library, television room, and study. I climbed a
cedar staircase wide enough to hold the whole
Balmain pack. There were five bedrooms on the
second floor. Sir Phil had the pick of the crop—a
big, high-ceilinged chamber with double French
windows letting onto a wide balcony. He had a
big, high bed covered with a tapestry that
seemed to depict some major military event.
Maybe one of his wives had found herself with
time on her hands.

The other rooms weren't much. The smallest
of them wasn't more than about twice the size of
my bedroom in Glebe. One of them had evidently been occupied by a woman.

There was a soiled feminine silk dressing
gown hanging on the back of the door and several items of makeup lay scattered on top of a
chest standing beside a full-length mirror. Unlike
the other rooms I'd seen in the house, this one
was dusty and untidy—books on the floor beside
the roughly made bed, a hairbrush and a coffee
mug on the dresser. I made a thorough search
but found nothing—no letters under loose floorboards, no photograph taped to the back of the
mirror, no nightclub book matches. Very little
scope for detecting. The hairbrush was almost
the only thing worth looking at. It held several

very long strands of very blond hair. The room looked like a place to crash rather than to live in.

I went up a smaller staircase to the top level. The attic rooms were used for storage. Tea chests, cardboard boxes, and old furniture lay around, wearing an air of rejection. I pushed my way through to the window of the room on the right side of the house, rubbed dust from the pane, and looked out. I could see all the way over the slate, tile, and iron rooftops to Coogee. Under a clear sky the water was a deep tourist-attracting blue, and sunlight bounced off the buildings along the foreshore. Somehow it was natural to look at the distant seascape, an automatic response, but the foreground was just as pleasing. Most of the houses and streets boasted luxuriant trees, and the recent rain had given the area a lush, pampered look. The elevation was ideal. I scanned the streets to the west and north, then moved to the other room and surveyed the scene in the other directions. No tall, loose-limbed blondes hanging about, no white Honda Civic.

"Find anything interesting?" Sir Phillip Wilberforce said when I rejoined him in the solarium. This time I'd removed my leather jacket.

"Yes and no. You're very free with your house. I'm a total stranger."

He smiled and removed a mobile telephone from underneath the cane lounge. "I checked on you while you were up there, Mr. Hardy. If there had been any reason for concern, I would have had help by the time you came down."

"I'm impressed," I said.

"So am I. I was contemplating asking you what this exercise was going to cost me, but my information is that you are relatively honest."

"I could resent the 'relatively.'"

He shrugged and replaced the phone. "You have to allow for the natural resentment of public officials. The more intelligent of them know that outside their institutions they'd starve in the midst of plenty."

I might have agreed, partly, but he was starting to bore me. Rampant free enterprisers have only one song to sing. "When did you last see Paula?" I said.

He laughed. A million wrinkles broke out on his face and spread like ripples in a pool. "I'm not going to be questioned by you. Instead, answer this: How much would you accept to desist?"

I wiped my face with the back of my hand.

The shadows had advanced, but the solarium was still a hot box. "Sir Phillip," I said, "I *want* to desist. I've got other things to do. But I have to see her. Money doesn't enter into it."

"I hoped you'd say that." He was wearing his shades again. Now he took them off and gave me a blast from the Wilberforce baby blues. "I haven't seen my daughter for some weeks. She's the only one of my children I care a damn about. I'll pay you five thousand dollars, Mr. Hardy, to find her."

6

THERE'S NOTHING IN THE COMMERCIAL
Agents and Private Enquiry Agents Act to say
you can't take on two important cases at the
same time. It's not usually a sensible thing for a
one-man show to do, but this was different. I was
going to be looking for Paula Wilberforce anyway, and she'd already cost me money. Besides, I
was coming to like Sir Phil. There was something about his don't-give-a-damn attitude that
appealed to me, especially when it was com-

bined with some genuine concern. That was showing now.

"Poor little Paula. I don't pretend to have been a good father, Mr. Hardy. Do you have children yourself?"

"No."

"You need a lot of luck to bring it off. I had the devil's own luck in business but none at all in my personal life."

I sat down again. It was still hot in the solarium. Sweat was rolling off me. A little had collected in the thin folds of fat around the old man's waist; otherwise he was bone dry.

"You might say I worked harder at the one than the other, and that might be true. Who knows? When the pulse of life is throbbing, you don't step back to consider such things."

"I suppose not. Tell me, has she ever been suicidal?"

"Not to my knowledge. Why?"

I considered telling him then what his daughter had of mine. I rejected the idea. Why worry him further? I covered up by saying that it was impossible to stop a genuine suicide and quoting the statistic on the estimated number of missing people who had killed themselves. They're the ones who do it for themselves, not to make a show, and they don't care if their bodies are never found.

He listened, then shook his head. "Destructive, yes, but not self-destructive. She has an enormous ego. When she was young, it sometimes seemed as if there weren't enough books for her to read, words to learn, places to go."

"Maybe you should take your own advice. Just leave her alone."

"No. I can't do that. You seem a capable sort of fellow. Perhaps you could talk some sense into her. Paula never believed that I cared for her. Giving her things obviously didn't change her opinion. Perhaps hiring your services might."

Tricky country, that. But I could use the fee and I *needed* to find her quickly. To have her father's help and authority was a luxury. I said I'd accept his offer.

"Good. In the study desk you'll find a checkbook. Bring it out here, please, and we'll get things on a business footing."

I got the checkbook. The stubs suggested that the account was in the black to the tune of ten grand. He lowered it by one. He was showing signs of fatigue, but he gave me a quick rundown on Paula which didn't add much to what I already knew. She wasn't close to any of her half or stepsiblings. She had had a succession of boy-friends when she was younger but no one impor-tant in recent times.

"Would she have many possessions—books, furniture, clothes?"

"Heaps, in each category."

"Too much to carry around if she's staying with friends or living in motels?"

"Absolutely."

"Where would it all be?"

"In the Lindfield house, I imagine. To answer your earlier question, Paula has no right to sell it, but I suppose I would agree if it came to the point. I have a set of keys."

The keys were in the same desk drawer. Very orderly man, Sir Phil. I got his phone number, promised to stay in touch, and we shook hands. His dry hand was almost cold in my hot, moist one. I wondered what that meant.

Crisscrossing Sydney again by car. Not my favor-ite occupation, but it comes with the job. There was a long delay on the bridge approach because of roadworks, and the traffic remained slow and sticky for most of the way through Willoughby. At least I had a client to charge the petrol to.

Lindfield looked as self-assured and well paid up as ever. I parked directly outside the house and marched straight up the path to the front door, jiggling the keys in my hand. The garden was definitely overgrown, with weeds sprouting and several shrubs growing ragged. The neighbors would soon be getting up a committee to complain.

The house had a solid, respectable feel from the heavy front door through to the glassed-in back sunporch. There were three bedrooms. The largest, in the front to the right of the hall, was dark and furnished with the kind of stuff that is old, expensive, and depressing. The one opposite it was brighter and had been used as a kind of studio. It had drop cloths covering the carpet, and there were framed canvases, pencil and charcoal sketches on heavy paper, and enlarged photographs scattered about. The third bedroom, off the kitchen, was empty with a door that stuck on the frayed carpet.

I gave most of the house a quick once-over. The kitchen was old-style, but functional; the bathroom and toilet likewise. The dining room featured more of the heavy Victorian furniture but was enlivened by a few paintings on the walls. They were landscapes and sea studies, full of light and life. All unsigned.

The occupied bedroom had been cleaned of all signs of use. The drawers in the dresser and bedside table were empty, with fresh paper liners; the wardrobe was the same with only a few wire hangers taking up the space. I looked under the bed and under the mattress. Nothing. There was a film of dust over the surfaces, but no one had written any messages in it. An elaborately carved chair with a straight high back sat in a corner of the room and seemed to reproach me.

I went back to the studio. Here at least, something had gone on. It was past midday, and the light was fading in the room, but it must have been glorious earlier on. The bleached look of the drop cloths confirmed this. A tall easel had been laid on its side along one wall. I examined it and found that one of its legs was a splintered, fractured ruin. I found a mark on the wall where the easel had probably struck when it was hit or kicked. There were also paint smears, suggesting that a painting had flown off the easel and hit the wall. Which painting? A frame lying facedown was a mess; the wood was broken on two sides, and there were signs that a canvas had been cut and ripped out of it. The other framed pictures, more landscapes, showed no signs of disturbance.

They and the sketches were all unmistakably in the style of those on the dining room walls. Some of the drawings were barely begun; others had been left half finished. I'm no art critic, but these looked accomplished. I turned the heavy sheets of paper over, hoping to learn something. The only thing that struck me was the absence of human faces and figures. That seemed odd, but what do I know? A couple of studies of dogs, stretched out at a full run, had the kind of lifelike quality and vigor that someone like me who can't draw can only gape at.

Two things caught my eye simultaneously: a photograph, blown up to poster size, which looked to have been attacked by a paintbrush, and movement in front of the house. I picked up the creased and crumpled photograph and moved to the window. I could see clearly through the greenery to the street. A police car had pulled up behind mine. Two officers approached the Falcon. One carried a clipboard. He consulted it and checked my registration number. He nodded to his mate, who went back to their car. I couldn't see what he was doing, and I didn't want to wait around to find out. I had no outstanding traffic infringements, so my rego number was on their list for another reason. After a second or two they advanced on number 12. One made as if to draw his pistol. The other stopped him, but one trigger-prone cop is more than enough.

I shot through the house, checked that I had the keys and that I hadn't left anything lying around. I bounded down the back steps and flipped the door shut behind me. The backyard was short. I was at the fence in a couple of strides and over it with an agility that surprised me. I found myself in a large garden with a sprinkler system playing. I dodged the sprays and made it across to the fence on the right. Over that without damage. Still no dogs. I skulked through shrubberies and climbed fences in an easterly direction for a couple of hundred yards. Eventually, more by luck than good management, I dropped into a lane that led to a street. I emerged from my multiple trespasses without the faintest idea where I was.

I was panting as I turned into Tryon Road, which gave me some idea of my whereabouts. I straightened my clothes and tried to look as if I belonged there. To my surprise, I still had the photograph clutched in my right hand. I folded it and put it in my pocket. Then it was a matter of making my way to a main road and hailing a cab. I tramped for a mile or so of more leafy streets before I reached the Pacific Highway. It was getting close to three o'clock, when the taxi drivers change shifts and want to head for home or base. I walked along the road for twenty minutes before I got a driver to stop. I said, "Glebe" automatically and only began to think as we approached the Gladesville Bridge.

There had to be some kind of bulletin out on me and my car. The cops had checked the license plate, then checked with HQ, and it couldn't have been just a parking fine or to tell me that Glen had been in a car accident because one had touched his gun. The hunt would be on seriously now that I'd skipped out on that pair. The question was, What had I done? I couldn't think of anything in recent times. That left only one explanation: Paula Wilberforce had done something she shouldn't have with my .38.

I got the driver to drop me at the bottom of Glebe Point Road, and I climbed to the top of one of the blocks of flats behind my street, one of those that impede my view of Blackwattle Bay. I had a clear sight up and down the street, and I knew by heart the cars that usually parked there at this time of the day. The gray Laser was definitely out of place. No food for the cat tonight. I needed a drink and a place to sit and think. I knew I should go to the cops myself, but something about those two with their shiny boots and pistols made me think twice. My profession wasn't in good odor with the constabulary at the best of times, and these times were not that good. A couple of PEAs had been in the news lately, both acquitted of conspiracy charges on account of tainted police evidence.

My office was out, obviously. The only other place I could think of was Glen's flat, which they might visit but where they probably wouldn't kick the door down. I hopped on a bus that took me to Parramatta Road and caught another one up as far as Norton Street. Glen's flat was close to Fort Street High School, and a few stragglers dressed in motley versions of the school uniform and carrying khaki bags that looked as if they had done service in World War II dawdled along the streets. Caution was becoming second nature. I skulked at one end of the street, watching the human and vehicular traffic. Nothing out of the ordinary—no one hanging about in front of Glen's block, no occupied parked cars, no helicopters overhead.

I had a key to Glen's place as she had to mine, the only difference being that I'd never used it. The block was on three levels, one below the street. Glen had told me she was in the street-level section, which was reached by a kind of bridge running above the basement flats to the pavement. There was no security door. I went across the bridge and into the dark lobby and quickly up a flight of stairs. No one lurking or challenging. I went in and felt safe for the first time in a couple of hours. My first need was for a drink. Glen's indifference to alcohol is a source of wonder to me. She simply doesn't care whether she has any or not. But she was well enough supplied with what she favors when she does drink—gin and white wine. I poured a generous slug of gin over ice and sat down to do some thinking.

The cold gin relaxed me. The telephone rang twice, but I didn't answer it. I took a look out of the window from time to time, but the street was quiet. I wandered around the flat, feeling like an intruder. I recognized some of the things Glen had brought from her house at Whitebridge: a pine table, a leather couch, and a couple of paintings. The pictures reminded me of the photograph in my pocket. I sat down at the table and smoothed it out. At first I thought it was some kind of abstract study, but as I looked closer, I could make out a face and the upper part of a man's naked body. The features were almost obliterated, by either the film's being wrongly exposed or a deliberate artistic device. The slashes of paint across the surface didn't help.

I had another drink and stared at the picture. I wondered if I'd be able to recognize the person if I met him. Large or small, young or old, fair or dark, it was hard to say. There was no sense of perspective. The face was arresting though with a suggestion of . . . what? Strength? Madness? For whatever reason, the photograph had clearly meant something to whoever had painted in the studio of the Lindfield house. Who was that? Paula Wilberforce herself? I had no way to know. I refolded the picture and put it back in my jacket, which was now hanging over a chair. It was getting cold in the flat. I turned on an electric radiator and began to feel drowsy. No good. I turned the radiator off and tried to get on with my thinking.

Nothing much came except a decision that what I did next would be governed by what

Paula Wilberforce had done. Reactive thinking, but the best I could do. I contemplated another drink but decided that contacting Glen in Goulburn would be a better idea.

7

GLEN ANSWERED IMMEDIATELY. "CLIFF, what in God's name have you been doing?"

"For the last couple of hours I've been hiding from your colleagues. Have they been on to you?"

"I'll say. I was plucked out of a meeting and practically given the third degree about you."

"I'm sorry, love. What's it all about?"

It was a key question, and everything would depend on how she answered it. I swilled the dregs of the gin and melted ice, and the pause seemed to go on forever.

"All they told me is that there's been a shooting. Someone was wounded. Your car was seen nearby."

"Wounded? Not killed?"

"Wounded. Cliff—"

"Who? Where?"

"Christ, Cliff, I tell you I don't know. An old man. In Randwick somewhere. What . . ."

I told her about it in as much detail as I could muster there and then. It was a relief to tell it. "I hope the old guy's okay," I said. "What about the gun?"

"I don't know."

"If she's still got it, I'm in the shit."

"Cliff, you have to go in. Why don't you ring Frank Parker? He'll smooth things out for you. Where are you calling from?"

My mind was racing: Even if Frank Parker could ensure me a reasonable hearing, it was likely that my license would be suspended. I would probably be watched. What chance would I have of finding Paula Wilberforce then? And there was the matter of the bullets posted to Mount Victoria. She might even have seen where the package was going. I couldn't explain all that to the cops, nor could I sit back and let things take their course.

"Cliff?"

"I can't go in," I said. "It's too tricky. I've got something else that can't wait."

"Something else, my God! What could be more important than this?"

"Life and death," I said.

"Cliff, are you drunk?"

I almost told her that I'd buy her a new bottle of gin, but I managed not to. "I'm not drunk. Listen, Glen, I've got things to do—"

"Are you mad? There's an APB out on you."

I laughed. Maybe I *was* a bit drunk; two very stiff gins on a very empty stomach can do it. "I've had those things out on me before. They won't shoot on sight, will they?"

"Don't joke, Cliff. Where are you?"

"Sorry. It's better that you don't know."

"I want to help. Frank will too. We *can* help."

"I don't think so. Not just now. When will you be home?"

"Tonight, of course. I'm coming straight back."

I didn't say anything, and it hit her that I wasn't going to be around.

Her voice faltered. "I . . . You don't trust me."

"It's not that. You'd have to turn me in. You'd be in the shit yourself if you didn't. This is my trouble."

"You're behaving like an idiot."

"I've got to go. I'll call you at home later." I hung up and breathed out slowly. I'd just avoided saying "here" instead of "at home." Terrific. Now I had trouble on four fronts: Wilberforce, Lamberte, the New South Wales police, and Glenys Withers. Plus I'd given a terrible lecture and didn't have a car. It would have to rate as one of my more inglorious days.

I turned on the TV for the six o'clock news. It had been a slow day, and the shooting made an item: "A man was shot today at his home in Randwick." The screen showed the house and some paramedics toting a stretcher toward an ambulance. "Neighbors of Sir Phillip Wilberforce, a retired businessman, say they heard muffled noises that seemed to come from inside this large house. Then there was a clearer noise that sounded like a shot. There was some delay before anyone investigated and Sir Phillip was found beside his swimming pool bleeding from a wound. A spokesman for the Prince of Wales

Hospital said that on account of Sir Phillip's age, his condition was being classified as critical. A blue Falcon sedan was observed near the house, and police are anxious to interview the driver." There was a quick take of a police detective staring up at the house and then one of the solarium and one of bloodstains on the tiles around the pool. The ambulance drove away.

It was less than helpful. I still didn't know how badly the old fellow had been hit or whether the police had found the gun. Glen would find those things out for sure, and maybe she would tell me. It wouldn't take long to drive from Goulburn so my bolt-hole had a limited life. I had a shower, made coffee, and ate two cheese sandwiches made with stale bread. I looked at the gin and Riesling, but I was strong. Then I sat down and wrote a note to Glen saying that I loved her and trusted her and needed her help. I thought about telling her about the Lamberte case but decided against it.

I didn't want to leave. Glen's odors, familiar and pleasing, were in the air. I opened her bedroom and looked at the bed. Inviting. I wondered when we'd get a chance to use it, if ever. I sensed that I was on dangerous ground with Glen now, and there would be more trouble to come unless things straightened out quickly. The thought struck me that she might have her service pistol here and that I might need it. I swore at myself, closed the bedroom door, and left the flat.

I rang Terry Reeves from a public phone, not wanting to use Glen's resources any more than I already had, a worrying state of affairs. Terry had expanded his car rental business since I'd helped him out a few years back, when someone had been stealing his cars. Now he also rents four-wheel drives, camping and skiing gear, and other things for people whose idea of fun is to put themselves through discomfort. He lives in a terrace opposite his business operation so he can watch over it personally. He also has several thousand dollars' worth of alarm systems installed. I'd solved Terry's immediate problem, but last I'd heard, his paranoia had got worse. He stayed open until he was absolutely sure that no one was going to wander in to rent a Jackaroo and a tent.

A tired-sounding female receptionist put me through to Terry.

"Are you still driving that bloody Falcon, Cliff?" he said.

"Same car, later model, but I'm . . . ah, temporarily without wheels."

"I can sell you a Subaru. Ex-fleet but the cleanest, sweetest—"

"No, Terry. I want to rent something. I'll be over in a cab. Give me half an hour."

"Where are you? I'll pick you up."

"What? You can't knock off yet. It's only just gone seven."

"I'm getting help with all that. Trying not to be so obsessive."

"You? Not obsessive?"

"Yeah. I'm having therapy. C'mon, Cliff, give me a break. I'm trying to refocus."

"Jesus. I'm in Petersham. New Canterbury Road, corner of Crystal Street."

"What're you doing there?"

"Terry . . ."

"Okay. Stay put. I'm in a white Commodore."

A lot of cars went past as I waited near the corner. It was dark, and the warmth of the day had vanished. A cold wind blew along Crystal Street, carrying fast-food aromas, exhaust fumes, and dust. I was wearing a leather jacket, Levi's, a green corduroy shirt, cracked and battered Italian leather shoes. My heavy dark beard had sprouted since the none-too-close shave of that morning. I looked and felt like a suspicious character. A police car cruised by, and I had to steel myself not to shrink back into the shadows.

The white Commodore pulled up on the other side of the road, paused, and did a showy U-turn to end up immediately in front of where I was skulking. I leaped forward, wrenched open the door, and dived in.

"Shit, Terry," I said. "Why don't you try to make yourself conspicuous?"

He gunned the motor, waiting for another car to pull out around him. "Sorry, Cliff. I just feel so good."

I was pushed back against the well-padded seat as he accelerated away. "Terry," I said, "take it easy. You're a respectable businessman driving an accessory to Christ knows what."

He made the next turn on the amber light with screaming tires. "I don't care. I've got to feel loose."

"Fuck loose," I said, "I've got to feel safe."

"Put your seat belt on, then."

He drove in his expert, if sporty, manner through Stanmore toward Surry Hills.

"I heard you were shacked up with a female copper," he said as he passed the railway and entered Eddy Avenue.

"Right," I said.

Like most of my male friends, Terry had met and admired Helen Broadway. "The only cure for one woman is another woman," he said.

"Right," I said again.

"I want you to meet Wanda."

"Wanda?"

"My therapist put me on to her. It's fantastic. She's helped me enormously."

I leaned back against the padded seat and closed my eyes. "Good, Terry," I said. "I'm happy for you. I hope she hasn't turned you into a totally solid citizen."

"What's the trouble, Cliff?"

"You wouldn't want to know. But if you can fix me up with a four-wheel drive, a tent, and a Primus stove, it'd be a big help."

"Serious problems can't be solved by material things, mate."

"Terry," I said. "Don't. Just don't."

Wanda turned out to be a big blond woman of about Terry's age or a few years older. Everything about her shrieked "Mum," but Terry seemed to lap it up. He told her about how I'd cracked the stolen car racket and how I had a penchant for old Falcons with defective heaters and no cassette player. Wanda smiled indulgently at me and touched Terry every chance she got. They fed me on Wanda's vegetable soup and homemade bread, and then Terry took me across to the lot.

The staff had finally knocked off. It took Terry ten minutes to deactivate the alarm system. Wanda hadn't had any effect in that department. His operation had expanded since I'd last seen him. He had a big service area and an imposing customer lounge. There weren't many cars around, which I took to be a good thing, business-wise.

"I can let you have a Land Cruiser, Cliff. How long would you be wanting it?"

"A week at the most."

"That'll be okay. Did you say you wanted camping gear?"

"A bit. Nothing fancy."

"D'you want a mobile phone?"

An hour later I was on the road. I had a one-man tent, a groundsheet, foam rubber slab, sleeping bag, parka, thick gloves, tilly lamp, torch, binoculars, a Panasonic camera with zoom lens, Primus stove, matches, a thermos full of soup, and a half bottle of Johnnie Walker Red Label. The Land

Cruiser had a full tank of petrol and was running smoothly. I turned on the radio and caught the nine o'clock news, but there was nothing about Sir Phillip Wilberforce. I wondered how he'd made his money and how much there was of it. I could feel the folded photograph in my pocket. It was my only glimmer of a lead in the Wilberforce case. It would be useful to ask Sir Phil about it, Dr. John Holmes also, possibly. No chance of that for now.

I punched the radio buttons as I drove. The quiz on the ABC station held me for a few minutes when I knew some of the answers and lost me when I didn't. I ran through a blizzard of commercials, religion, and talk-back until I got Beethoven's *Emperor* Concerto on FM. It's one of the few classical pieces I can listen to without drifting off into thoughts carnal or mundane. The first movement, great stuff. I tapped my totally unmusical fingers on the steering wheel and began to feel better. The night was clear, and the traffic was light. The heater worked. I was heading for the pure, clean air of the Blue Mountains. If I'd had any solid idea of what I was going to do when I got there, I'd have felt almost in charge of my life.

8

I STOPPED AT EMU PLAINS AND BOUGHT some supplies at an all-night service station: bread, cheese, instant coffee, and milk. Also a detailed map of the Blue Mountains. I studied it carefully, approximately locating the Lamberte block. The four acres appeared to be well out of the town and reached by several roads of ever-decreasing importance. Verity Lamberte had mentioned Bell's Road and the railway. There was a valley between them and the block. The Electricity Commission had a track through it to service overhead power lines, and there were several fire trails.

It was cool in Emu Plains; it would be colder in the mountains. I filled a plastic water bottle I'd found in the back of the Cruiser. I bought a cup of coffee, spiked it with the whiskey, and sipped it slowly. When I couldn't put it off any longer, I called Glen on the mobile phone.

"I got your note," she said quietly. "Thank you."

"I'm sorry. I think this is the way to do it."

"It's not. You're being stubborn and stupid. Where the hell are you now? Not that you'll tell me."

"Glen, all the explaining, the paperwork, the sitting about would take up days. I've got things to do. If nothing works out, I'll come in. I promise."

"Meanwhile, that crazy woman is running around with your gun."

"So she's still got the gun, has she?"

"Yes. How many rounds were in it?"

"Eight."

"Terrific. She put one in her dad and shot off another six or seven."

"Which? Six or seven?"

"They don't know. D'you see, Cliff? She might have one bullet left."

"Shit." The phone buzzed with static.

"Cliff! Cliff! What's all that? Are you using a car phone?"

"Yes. How's Wilberforce?"

"Weak, in and out of it. But they say he'll pull through. Seems to be a tough old bird. It's a weird family, but I suppose you know that."

"No, I know bugger all about them. This whole thing has just sort of blown up around me. I can tell you one thing: Wilberforce hired me to find his daughter."

"You don't say. Big news. They found the checkbook. They're not totally stupid. But finding a check stub made out to you for a grand hasn't exactly helped you so far, Cliff."

"Look, love, I just can't be of any use right now. If I could talk to Wilberforce . . ."

I let it hang there. She didn't respond. We both knew that there was no way to bring that off. I could feel her hostility and anger. Telephones don't facilitate calm and understanding.

"That means you *have* got some ideas. Please, Cliff, let me come and see you. We can talk—"

"No, Glen. Give me a couple of days."

"To do what, where, for Christ's sake? Do you know who I feel like? Who I sympathize with?"

"Tell me."

"Your poor starving fucking cat!"

She hung up. I clutched the dead handset and looked out through the windshield at the highway. I could pull out onto it and head back to the city. Talk to Glen, get into bed with her. Do a deal with Detective Inspector Somebody-or-Other in the morning. Tell them what little I knew. Get myself sidelined. I couldn't do it. I started the engine and headed for the mountains. Every mile produced a new rationalization and justification. No one could talk to Wilberforce until he was better; therefore, the photograph wasn't any use. Paula had either one round in the .38 or none. If none, fine; if one, she might not even know about it. If she did know, she'd probably think long and hard about using it. Wouldn't she?

I remember seeing a miniseries in which Michael York played a German doctor who'd been forced to do bad things by the Nazis. He'd got to Australia illegally and was working in a Gippsland timber camp. The script forced him into utterances like "Der air is like vine." By Blackheath the mountain air was like wine all right, but very cold wine. There was an almost full moon, no clouds, and a strong, chilly wind. I stopped for a piss in a public toilet, and the wind cut straight through my jacket and shirt. It seemed like a long time since I'd been out of the city, and despite my problems, it was exhilarating to feel the mountains all around, with more trees than houses and the sky huge and clear overhead.

There was almost no traffic on the road on the rest of the drive up to Mount Victoria. I shut down the heater because it made me drowsy. I turned off the radio as well and denied myself the swig on the whiskey I would have welcomed. This was no holiday, no pleasure jaunt. Unless I was smart and careful, I'd be spotted immediately, transported to Sydney, and subjected to that peculiar skepticism that cops acquire through their mother's milk or start learning from their first day on the job.

Mount Victoria was still and quiet. The last train had left, and the lights were out in the pub and the couple of large guesthouses on the edge of the town. The residents were inside around their fires and potbelly stoves and TV sets. The blue light outside the nice old double-fronted police station was glowing, but the building was in darkness. I rolled on through and took the Mount York Road. All street lighting ceased after two more right turns, and then I was on the thin, rutted track called Salisbury Road that ran past the Lamberte holding.

A square block of four acres gives you a frontage of roughly two hundred yards; I retained that much from high school arithmetic. The lots along Salisbury Road were at least that size or possibly bigger. It was hard to tell because some were vacant, others had houses set well back from the road, and in most cases there were only hand-painted signs tacked on to trees to indicate where properties began and ended. I used the spotlight mounted on the roof sparingly even though it looked like weekender territory. The track didn't get a lot of work, and the entrances to the blocks had that half-grown-over look that indicates occasional use.

The Lamberte lot was no exception. There was a wire fence running along the front perimeter, but one of the strands had snapped; several of the posts had sagged inward, and the fence looked halfhearted. The track onto the block was marked by a gnarled eucalypt which had "Lambert" painted on it, evidently executed by someone other than the owner. Unfamiliar as I was with the area and dark as the tree-lined track was, the Lambertes seemed to have the best of the location. I stopped at the last fence post and looked across the valley. In the far distance I could see the lights of the Bell's Road and imagine where the railway must run. *Very nice, Patrick*, I thought. *If I were in the asset-hiding business, this would definitely be one to hide.*

The nearest neighbor was the better part of a mile away. I could see the back of the house nestled down among a stand of trees, on a rock shelf fifty yards from the road. No lights, no sign of a vehicle. I was tempted to break in and toss the place. You never knew, maybe Mr. Patrick Lamberte had a shelfful of wife-murder books: *The Memoirs of Dr. Crippen*, *The True Life Story of John Christie*, *Tony Agostino Tells All*. I resisted the impulse, recognizing it as unprofessional and sloppy. Besides, I was in enough trouble already without adding a break-and-enter charge.

I drove on to where the Electricity Commission track met Salisbury Road. It hadn't been used for some time, and the bush was fighting back, trying to reclaim the cleared space. That suited me. I engaged the four-wheel drive and piloted the Land Cruiser slowly along the track, probing ahead with my lights on full beam. I didn't want to break an axle on a creekbed or rip a tire to shreds on a metal stake. But the saplings parted easily, brushing the windows on both sides, flicking at the windshield, and the fall of the land was gentle. The map suggested the presence of a fire trail running to the right, behind the Lamberte land, but it was too dark to search for it. After the hectic events of the day, the sudden slowing down of movement, the dark, and the quiet hit me and let me know how close to exhaustion I was. I could scarcely hang on to the wheel as the tires bumped along in old, hard-baked ruts. The bush on either side hemmed me in; tall trees shut out the moonlight.

I slowed to a crawl and pulled off the track into the trees. Within a few yards the front bumper came to rest against a solid trunk, and that was far enough. I killed the lights and waited for a time to make sure my arrival in the valley hadn't attracted any attention. A couple of wallabies thumped in the bush nearby, and some night birds whistled and cooed. By torchlight I emptied my bladder into a fern bush and made my bed in the back of the Cruiser—foam rubber unrolled, sleeping bag spread out, the parka for a pillow, off with the jacket and shoes, a big swig of whiskey to clean the clackers, and good night.

I woke up a few minutes before dawn, that time when the temperature seems to drop suddenly by a couple of degrees. Inside the sleeping bag, with my jeans, shirt, and socks on, I was frozen. My breath was like a fog machine in action, and when I reached out for my watch, I touched metal that stung. It was no hardship to get up and moving. I climbed into my jacket and pulled on the parka, the gloves, and the hiking boots, and I was still cold. I stamped around in the almost-light, flapping my arms and taking deep breaths of the icy air.

The sun came up, and it got slightly warmer immediately. The Cruiser started at the first turn of the key. I backed out of my shelter and began to search for the fire trail. There was a deep frost but only a light mist. The exhaust was sending up clouds of steam. I spotted the narrow, muddy trail and turned onto it. A small creek trickled over rocks and followed the track for a few yards before changing course and running downhill. I stopped at a point I judged to be directly below the Lamberte place. The tree cover had been thinned over the years under the power lines, and I had a good view of the country above me. Glass winked in the sunlight to the left. I drove on another twenty yards and swept the hill with the binoculars. I was slightly past the house and a hundred yards below it. Above me was a jumble of rocks that seemed to join up with the rocky shelf on which the cabin sat.

I parked between two big trees; the exhaust steam faded away, and the bush noises took over: birdcalls, the wind in the trees, running water. My teeth were chattering, and my fingers were stiff with cold inside the thick gloves. Wanda's soup was still warm. I drank almost all of it and ate several slices of bread. I boiled water on the Primus and made instant coffee. Then I slung the binoculars around my neck and began to climb the rock pile. It was steeper and harder than it looked from below. After a few minutes I was hot and discarded the parka. The hiking boots were well used, comfortable and gave a good purchase on the damp rocks. A sheer-faced ten-yard-high boulder forced me to move to my left, and when I went around it I found myself on a ledge about seventy-five yards west of and slightly above the Lamberte cabin.

There was light timber between me and it, but

the powerful Zeiss glasses gave me an excellent sight of the back of the house. I squatted and regained my breath. The position could hardly have been better. I could see the track all the way up to the road. Near the house there was a cleared space where cars could be parked; wood was stacked under the jutting eaves, and the barbecue area was handy but a safe distance from the building. The water tank was in view, and beyond it, connected to the house by a cable, was a small shed which almost certainly housed the generator. The cabin was nicely sited, with a view out over the valley. I couldn't see it, but I'd have been willing to bet that the place had a front deck, possibly cantilevered out over the rock shelf. No self-respecting architect could do otherwise.

I scratched under my chin where the stubble was beginning to itch and thought about my next move. If Lamberte met with anyone up here and any weapons were displayed, I'd be able to get pictures. It was a pity that I didn't have any bugging equipment. I had the gear at my place in Glebe, but that was no doubt being watched around the clock by the constabulary. Lamberte was due to arrive today, and I'd have to be at the post office when it opened to hang around to see whether he picked up the package. Doing that without attracting attention to myself was going to be tricky. It was nicer out here, with the birds whistling and the steam rising off the rocks as the sun climbed above the trees.

I stared down at the house, and again I was tempted. What harm could it do, a little look around? From what Verity Lamberte had said it didn't sound as if the place were used all that often. So what if I disturbed the kindling box or left the Trivial Pursuit set slightly off line? Who'd notice? I've never owned a country house or a weekender, but I was pretty sure that if I did, I'd make certain the lights were out and the stove was off and that's about all I'd worry about before the next visit. A place to slob about in, leave things lying comfortably around. Wasn't that the point?

I was measuring the distance and thinking about hopping over a rocky outcrop and sliding down a lightly timbered slope when I was saved from folly. A Land Rover came chugging in from the road and negotiated the track down to the parking spot in front of the woodpile. A man got out. He was tall and trimly built, wearing country clothes—jeans, boots, heavy sweater—that managed to look at once smart and fashionable. He fitted the description Verity Lamberte had given me of her husband: tall and well built with graying brown hair, receding at the temples.

It was his attitude that clinched the identification for me, though. He looked utterly at home, completely proprietorial. People who own country land tend to behave as if their title extended over everything they survey—far out to sea if they occupy a coastal headland, to the horizon in the outback. Lamberte clapped his gloved hands together and stamped his feet. His breath plumed in the cold air. He talked animatedly and waved his hands about, while pointing in this direction and that. Then he went around to the other side of the Land Rover and opened the door. The woman he handed down was a tall blonde.

9

AT FIRST I THOUGHT IT WAS PAULA WILBER-
force, and I almost shouted with surprise. I did
make some kind of noise, and I pulled back fast
behind the nearest large rock. I recovered and
took a good look through the glasses. Lamberte
and the woman were unloading the back of the
Land Rover. She had the Wilberforce build and
hair; but her face was fuller, and she was a few
years older than Paula. The pair looked comfortable together, as if they'd done this sort of thing
many times before, which had to make you spec-

ulate about what else they'd done before. Lamberte unlocked the back door, and they ferried in their cardboard boxes, overnight bags, and bundles. Two trips each, and they were done. The door closed behind them. A short time later a puff of smoke issued from the chimney and made me realize how cold and lonely I was.

There was nothing to be gained by staying where I was. It was only just past seven o'clock, too early to start hanging around the post office. I stared at the cabin door, willing someone to come out, something to happen. Nothing did. I remembered Verity Lamberte's statement about Patrick: "He's a very attractive man physically. He knows it and uses it." that was what he was doing right now. He wasn't likely to come out and start chopping wood. I scrambled back down the rocks, timing myself. It took about four minutes to get down, maybe twice that long to get up. So what? I didn't know. It was just something to do.

Anyway, it seemed like a safe time to move the Land Cruiser. I drove back along the fire trail toward the service track. As near as I could judge, I couldn't be seen from the cabin. When I reached the service road, I turned in the other direction and did a little exploring. There were several tracks through this part of the valley, and one led up to the highway. So there were two ways into my spy point. I tried to make finding that out feel like an achievement. I sneezed violently several times as I drove, and I could feel a cold building inside my head. Great for surveillance work.

I drove into town and killed time buying petrol, tissues, and a newspaper. There was a small item on the Wilberforce shooting. His condition was unchanged; the police still wanted to interview the driver of a Falcon seen in St. Marks Road some time before the shooting. I caught a glimpse of myself in the side mirror as I climbed back into the Cruiser. My hair was wild, and I had a heavy growth of dark beard sprinkled with gray. I sneezed, swore, and wiped my nose savagely. My eyes were red and wet-looking.

"You're getting too old for this," I said.

"I beg your pardon?" A woman crossing the road looked at me oddly, and I realized that I had spoken aloud.

I sneezed and grinned at her, no doubt a horrible sight. "Nothing," I said. "Talking to myself."

She gave me a tentative smile and very deliberately moved a little farther away as she passed.

I didn't blame her. I was parked outside the post office at nine o'clock on the dot. It was an old building set on a rise above the highway with the Imperial Hotel and the Bells Road turnoff opposite. There was a general store a little farther along and an "old wares" shop. The post office opened at five past nine, but business was slow. A woman from the antiques shop took in a few parcels; a couple of elderly people made heavy weather of the climb but emerged with envelopes and contented expressions. I sat behind my paper, sneezing and feeling conspicuous. Balmain had won an interstate night game; Wimbledon was shaping like an all-European final, again; rail fares were up, air fares were down.

Patrick Lamberte drove up and parked behind me. I used the last of my pocket pack of tissues as he walked into the post office. He was an impressive figure: six feet or so and trim. He'd changed his sweater; otherwise he looked pretty much as he had when I'd first seen him except that he was wearing a satisfied, just-had-a-great-fuck look. For a man supposedly facing bankruptcy, he seemed remarkably chipper. When he came out of the post office, he was carrying a couple of letters and a parcel, about the size of a paperback book, wrapped in brown paper. He tossed it up once and caught it deftly before he swung himself inside the Land Rover. I wiped my running nose on the sleeve of my parka and hated him.

He jumped in and gunned the Land Rover up the hill toward Mount York Road. I followed sedately, wishing that I'd bought more tissues and cold tablets and Strepsils and rum. I had learned absolutely nothing from Lamberte's manner. My tentative judgment was that his air of self-satisfaction was probably so strong and so constant that it would always be hard to tell what he was thinking or feeling. He drove fast, bullying a couple of slower cars and changing into the right-turn lane at precisely the moment calculated to cause most consternation behind him. I followed until I was sure that he was headed toward Salisbury Road without any stops along the way and then turned off to take my alternative route into the valley.

The head cold was making my ears ring, and my throat felt like Velcro. I was coughing and sniffling when I reached the bottom of the stack of rocks that ascended to my vantage point.

"Twenty-four-hour cold, Cliff," I said. "Treatment: exercise, vitamin C, and alcohol."

I was talking to myself again and beginning to feel light-headed. I grabbed the glasses and the whiskey and began to climb the rocks. Sweat broke out on me almost at once; it ran into my eyes, and I had to stop to wipe them. I took off the parka and tied its sleeves around my waist. I suppressed a giant sneeze and went on with the climb. My thin city socks weren't right for the boots, and I could feel blisters building on each heel. I made it to the ledge and rewarded myself with a swig on the Johnnie Walker. It seemed to clear my head. I moved forward, lifted the glasses, and peered at the cabin. The Land Rover was sitting in its spot by the woodpile. Smoke was drifting lazily from the chimney. *They're probably having coffee*, I thought, *and getting ready for a rematch, no holds barred*. I lowered the glasses. At that instant there was a roar like a low-flying jet and the back of the cabin burst into flames. I dropped the binoculars, jumped across a yard of open space to a big rock, scrambled over that, and took off toward flatter ground that would take me to the house. I ran, jumped, and scrambled, pushing through low bushes and slipping and sliding on damp grass. A window cracked, and the flames roared from it, withdrew, then shot out more fiercely than before. I kicked at the back door until it splintered, but the flames flared around the broken panels and drove me back. There was a hose running from the water tank. I turned it on and played it around the door, but it had no effect. I ran around the side of the house, looking for another way in or out, but the windows were all set high in the timber walls, which were already smoking.

I untied the parka, soaked it, and held it over my head as I rushed along the front deck, where the heat was less fierce. I kicked in a window and went through it into a big room that was filled with acrid, lung-searing smoke. I saw movement over toward a half-open door and lunged forward. The woman was in the full regalia—black neck ribbon, bra, garter belt, and stockings—and all of it, like her cloud of blond hair, was on fire. I grabbed her, beat at the flames with the wet parka, but she pushed me away.

"Patrick!" she screamed. She moved toward the door, which was gushing smoke and fire.

"Don't." My chest filled with smoke as I yelled, and I almost collapsed. I grabbed her arm and pulled her away from the door. She fought me. She was frantic and incredibly strong. Her mouth was open, and she was gulping down smoke as she sobbed and screamed. The roof beams were on fire above our heads, steaming and spitting out hot liquid, and the sea grass matting was burning under our feet. I clubbed her with a roundhouse swing, and she went limp. I extinguished the last of the burning hair and dragged her toward the window and the deck. She was big and a dead weight. Things were exploding into flames around me. I took a blow across the neck, and something seared my right shoulder.

The deck was burning. Its paint was blistering into bubbles and spurting little yellow and red flames. I dragged her through the fire and smoke and staggered blindly down the steps onto firm ground. The heat coming from the house was like a huge white-hot brick wall, threatening to fall on me. I couldn't see or breathe. I coughed and felt that I had expelled my lungs. Somehow I got to the running hose and sprayed water over the woman and myself. The shirt was burning on my back, and I screamed as I felt the flesh being grilled. The water cleared my vision. The hose came away from the tap, and I rolled under the gushing water, wallowing in the mud.

The woman lay on her back. She was naked now with bits of smouldering fabric sticking to her. Her eyes were closed. My hands were raw and felt useless as if I were wearing giant, flapping rubber gloves. The burned skin on my fingers was splitting. I tried to move her arms, to expand her chest. My strength was going, and I could scarcely move my limbs, let alone hers. I willed myself to do it: lift and open, lift and open. I thought about giving her the kiss of life, but her mouth was wide open, locked in a rictus of agony. I flapped her arms and felt the burned skin on my back peel and tear. She moaned and jerked, then went still.

I could hear the flames roaring in the trees around the front of the house. I looked up; a light wind was fanning the blaze, and the fire leaped from the house and caught on the canopy of the Land Rover. The interior of the vehicle filled with a bright red glow. I tugged at the woman and slid her through the mud, trying to get some shelter from the water tank. The Land Rover went up like an incendiary mine. Bits of metal clanged against the water tank and flew past me into the bush. The heat blast drove the air from my lungs, deafened and blinded me. I felt my hands slide from the woman's arm, the ground dissolved under me, and I disappeared into the middle of a blazing sun.

10

I DRIFTED AROUND TIMELESSLY IN A COUN-
try full of pain but devoid of responsibility. Only
sensations registered: warmth and cold, dryness
and damp, sound and quiet, hard and soft. I was
acutely aware of my body, of its shape and size,
its texture, and nothing else actually mattered.
There were visions—faces, voices, and vague
feelings of happiness or distress—but they were
nothing to do with me, not really. I was out of it
all, floating. Sometimes it seemed that I might
be going to land and the pain in every part of my

body would rise to an unbearable level and I would feel outraged that this could be happening. Not to me, not to the floating man. Then I would go aloft again, up into the stratosphere where everything was clean and cool and soft.

"Cliff, Cliff, darling. Can you hear me?"

It was Cyn's voice; no, Ailsa's; no, Ann's. No. It was Helen Broadway, and I hated her because she was pulling me in like a hooked fish. I wanted to stay out there in the cool cotton wool country, where nothing hurt and no one ever asked any hard questions like "Can you hear me?"

"Of course I can hear you," I said. "Go away. Let go, Helen. You didn't want me, not really. Don't . . ."

A woman's voice I didn't know, not quite, said, "Helen?"

"Helen Broadway," Frank Parker said. "Girlfriend. Before your time, Glen."

"Better be," Glen said.

I opened my eyes and saw them standing beside my bed. Frank Parker was wearing a blue suit. Glen had on a green dress.

"Colors," I said.

Glen leaned down and touched my face. "What?"

"I can see the colors."

Glen looked at Frank. "Should we get the doctor?"

Frank shook his head. I wondered what it would be like to shake my head, but it seemed like an impossibility. "They said he'd be vague for a while. He's taken an awful lot of dope."

"Who's a dope?" I said.

I felt something touch my hand and looked down. I supposed I had a hand, but just at present it looked like a bundle of white cloth. "You are," Glen said.

There were tears in her eyes, and I gathered something pretty important must have happened. Nothing seemed real. Little bits and pieces of my life and times came back to me in tantalizing snatches. I felt hot, and I itched all over. My mouth was dry. Then it hit me, all at once, just like that. The mountains, the house, the fire, and all the questions.

"How long?" I said.

Glen said, "Ten days."

"The woman?"

"She's dead, Cliff," Frank said, "along with

the man who was in the house. You bloody nearly went with them."

Glen seemed to sense what I needed. She poured some water from a carafe and held the glass to my lips. My hands were bandaged, and I could feel dressings on my face, shoulders, and back. "You had bad burns on your hands, face, and other bits," Glen said. "Also severe smoke inhalation. You had a temperature of a hundred and four."

"I was sick beforehand," I said. "Where am I now? Hospital at the Bay?"

Frank laughed. "You think you get freshly painted walls, TV, and young nurses there? You're in a private hospital in Petersham, near Glen's place."

I looked at Glen. She was pale and had lost weight. The last words I had heard from her were angry, but there was no sign of anger now. Something else. The look in her big eyes soothed me. Her mouth was slightly open, and I desperately wanted to kiss her. "All I can see is cops," I said. "Where's the young nurses?"

I fell asleep after that. This happened a few times over the following days. Glen would come in, tell me a little bit of the story, I'd feel better, then drop right back into nowhere land. It wasn't a bad way to live, all things considered. I was in a private room; the treatment I was getting was healing me fast, and Glen and I were getting along well in a quiet, foundation-building kind of way. But as I got a better grip on what had happened, the feeling of irresponsibility dropped away. When you feel you have to *do* something, your time as the pampered patient is at an end.

Patrick Lamberte had died in the fire. The woman whom I had tried to save was Karen Livermore, a dress designer aged thirty-eight. She was the sister of Verity Lamberte, my client. Patrick's wife. She was dead by the time the fire brigade arrived. The house had been completely destroyed, and I had been found near death and delirious. The police had discovered the Land Cruiser, identified me, and had questions to ask. I tried to contact my client, but her home number didn't answer, and all I could learn from her business associates was that she was "on leave." Glen and Frank fended their colleagues off for a time with the aid of the doctors, but eventually a Detective Sergeant Willis arrived with a police-woman carrying a laptop computer.

Willis was polite. He introduced himself and

Constable Booth and asked if I was prepared to make a statement.

"What about?" I said.

"The circumstances surrounding the fire at Salisbury Road, Mount Victoria, and the deaths of Patrick Lamberte and Karen Livermore."

I told it straight: why Mrs. Lamberte had hired me and what I'd done and hadn't done. I hadn't entered the cabin before the fire started; I hadn't actually seen Lamberte take the posted package inside; I had no idea of who the woman was and no brief to report on Patrick Lamberte's romantic associations. I didn't know where Mrs. Lamberte was now and had had no contact with her since the fire. Even when I ran dry, Willis didn't prompt me. Eventually I got through it all. Constable Booth had clattered away, easily keeping pace with me. She shut down her machine and told Willis she'd be back in an hour with a printout.

Willis, a tired-looking middle-aged man with jowls and thinning hair, flopped into a chair. "Doesn't sound too good," he said. "Even given the fuckin' stupid job blokes like you do."

I didn't say anything.

"You say you cleaned out the shells?"

I was tired by this time, and I simply nodded.

"Fits. They found a little lump of melted metal. What we don't know is what caused the fire. You reckon the wife set it up?"

I shrugged, hurting my burned back. "How would I know?"

"You've met her. You're her boy."

"Someone must have interviewed her by this time."

It was Willis's turn to shrug. "Not really. She was in shock, her quack said. She had a certificate. No one really got to talk to her. Now she seems to have pissed off. Sure you weren't rooting her yourself, Hardy?"

I closed my eyes.

"It's bad for you that she's not around. The sister shacked up with the husband?" Willis shook his head stagily. "Makes it hard to believe that you were camped out there in the fuckin' freezing cold just to keep an eye on things."

"I told you. She thought her husband was going to kill her."

"Nothing we've heard about him makes that likely. He was a wheeler-dealer and an arsehole, but that's it. And there again, he's not around to give your story the confirmation it so badly needs. You're in a bit of a spot, Hardy."

"What's the charge?"

"We could do something with putting dangerous materials through the post. Could cost you your license, but you've got a bit of pull, I hear. So maybe you can fancy step your way out of that."

I kept my eyes closed. His voice was a tired drone. With a bit of luck it'd send me off to sleep.

"Fire could've been an accident, I suppose," Willis went on. "Stove blew up as she was making cocoa. Or they were smoking in bed."

"There was an explosion."

"So you said. Then again, you were in the army. You probably know a bit about explosives and such."

"Not much."

"Still, you know the right people. Know someone who can take the bang out of bullets, for example. I'm not sure that's legal, and I don't think you happened to mention that person's name. Maybe he's got a workshop full of jelly and, what d'they call it, plastique?"

"You've seen too many movies. You're fishing. I'm tired. Go away, Sergeant."

Willis laughed. I opened my eyes as I heard his chair scrape on the floor. He'd pulled it closer to the bed, and now I could smell him: after-shave, bad teeth, and beer. "I'm sorry you're tired, Hardy, because that was just the easy part," he said. "You made your statement, and you'll sign it. Easy stuff. You were in control. You could lie as much as you liked. Thank Parker and your girlfriend for that. But their protection just ran out. Now I want to ask you a few questions, and you can take all the usual warnings as given."

I said, "About what?" But I knew.

"Tell me all about how this crazy twat who shot her dad got your gun and why you didn't say a fuckin' word about it."

Police minds work in strange ways. It seemed in this instance that they were more upset at my not reporting the loss of the pistol and evading their attempts to catch me than at a possible double murder. I said something like this to Willis.

"Don't kid yourself. It's early days in that investigation. If we come up with something against you, Hardy, you'll wish you'd taken up beekeeping."

Willis wasn't as jaded as he looked. He began to get worked up, and I wondered what lay behind his attitude. He'd been with me for almost two hours; maybe he found it hard to go that long without a drink. Maybe he didn't have private health insurance the way I had to have and resented my quiet room and leafy view. And there *were* young nurses. I wished one would come in now and usher him away. No such luck.

"I was embarrassed," I said. "It's embarrassing to have your gun lifted."

Willis snorted. "Especially by a woman."

"By anyone."

"And you're not embarrassed now? You can talk to me about it?"

I lifted my bandaged hands up above the blanket. The action hurt. "They tell me I nearly died. It puts things into perspective."

Willis scowled. "Fuckin' smart-arse private eyes," he said.

I twigged then. He was expressing the police force's anger over the publicity given to the case of two PEAs who'd been charged with bribing police officers, conspiracy to murder, and conspiring to pervert the course of justice. The case had been in the news when I'd made my trip to the mountains, but that was almost two weeks ago. Glen and I had talked about it in the early stages, but there must have been later developments which we hadn't discussed.

"Brewster and Loggins," I said. "What happened to them?"

Willis nodded. Some of the energy seemed to drain from him. "Loggins jumped bail. He's probably in Spain by now with that fuckin' . . ."

"Ray Brewster?"

"Offed himself. Took a uniformed man with him and left a letter."

There's nothing the police dislike more than suicide letters and dying declarations. They have a dramatic impact that is almost impossible to refute. I wondered what Brewster had said. I'd met him once—a big man, ex-cop, which made it worse, slow-witted and violent. He'd resigned from the force when it was obvious that he was on the take. The granting of a PEA license had been his price for keeping quiet about everyone else who was doing the same. An old story. Old pigeons coming home to an old roost.

"I've got nothing further to volunteer about the Wilberforce matter," I said. "Beyond this, I have a client whose interests I am pledged to protect."

"Get off the soapbox, you—"

There was a knock at the door, and Constable Booth entered carrying a sheaf of papers. She gave two sets to me and one to Willis as if she were unaware of the tension in the room. She wasn't, though. She clicked a ballpoint pen with perfect timing and handed it to me.

"A signature at the foot of two copies, please, Mr. Hardy. Sergeant Willis will witness. There are two passages which are a little obscure. I've tagged them. Perhaps you'd be good enough to make corrections and initial the two copies at those points."

"Happy to," I said.

I flicked through the pages slowly, trying not to let Willis see how much the movement hurt me, making the amendments and initialing, watching him do a slow burn. When we'd finished, Constable Booth executed a smart turn and marched from the room. Like me, she seemed to find the situation slightly ridiculous. I put my spare copy of the statement on the bedside cabinet, along with the water carafe, the as-yet-unopened paperbacks, and untouched grapes.

Willis heaved himself up from his chair. "Be careful," he said.

* * *

There had never been any question of skin grafts or plastic surgery. The burns, though severe, hadn't been the problem, nor the smoke inhalation. The thing that had laid me low was the pneumonia that had developed as a result of my severe cold plus the exertion, trauma, and exposure. I'd lain half naked in cold mud for some time before the rescuers had arrived. Antibiotics had knocked out the infection, but after twelve days in the hospital, I exhibited an allergic reaction to one of the drugs, and I went down again into a weakened state that had me sleeping around the clock and having disturbing dreams. I emerged from this bout clearheaded and alert but very weak physically.

Glen took me home to Glebe and stayed with me there. In one of my dreams I saw Sir Phillip Wilberforce stretched out on a morgue slab. I asked Glen for the latest on him.

"He pulled through," she said. "But he suffered some kind of stroke. I understand he's shaky all down one side, poor old bugger. He's at home, though. D'you want to send him a card?"

I was sitting in a deck chair in the back courtyard, soaking up winter sun. "I want to see him," I said.

"Why?"

"Remember he's my client too. Hired me to find his daughter Paula."

"Isn't that a conflict of interest? You're working for the Lamberte woman."

I shook my head. "The regulations are vague on this point. Hardy handles heavy caseload."

Glen grinned. "Fucks up all round."

"But soldiers on."

We looked at each other. Glen had taken leave, and we'd spent a week together, every night and a lot of the daytime. It was the longest time we'd put in like that apart from holiday breaks. It had worked well: a little gentle sex, taking care not to disturb my dressings and open my wounds; quiet walks; light meals; reading and watching TV together. We were closer than we'd ever been, each anticipating the other's wishes, responding to allusions, taking the hints. Great, and as artificial as a politician's smile.

"You're not ready," she said.

"I'm not planning to climb any mountains. I just want to move around a little. Talk to a few people."

"About what? I thought you didn't have any leads to follow."

"Why did you think that?"

"I just . . . never mind."

This was more like our usual style, slightly combative but mutually respectful, resolving itself in bed or being dissipated by work. We had both recognized that we worked different sides of the street. It made for a certain kind of tension that, I realized clearly then, I liked. I wasn't sure that Glen liked it as much.

I reached forward to touch her. We were sitting about a yard apart, and it felt like a mile or two. She didn't pull away, but the movement stretched the healed skin on my shoulders and made me wince. "Look, love," I said, "I don't believe those two died by accident."

"Your former client is being looked for. If you've got any information you should volunteer it."

"I haven't, but maybe if I just sniff around."

"Bullshit. And what did you say was your unstated motto: No dough, no show, wasn't that it?"

"All right, but the Wilberforce thing is different. She took my gun, for Christ's sake. I feel like a bloody idiot."

"Male pride. Terrific way to run a business."

"The old man . . ."

"Probably doesn't remember who you are. Leave it be, Cliff."

"And do what? Walk all the way to the library on my own? Read the TV listings? Pick a few winners and plan what to have for dinner?"

"Look at you. You can hardly move without something hurting."

"I want to find Paula Wilberforce. I *have* to. It's important."

"More important than your health? More important than me?"

"Shit."

The cat wandered out of the house, stood on the warm bricks, and stretched itself. It mewed and curled up in a corner. We both looked at it and laughed.

11

I STARTED BY GETTING MYSELF FIT ENOUGH to do more than get out of bed and feed the cat: long walks in the warm part of the day with my shirt off, up and down the Wigram Road hill several times a day, plenty of protein and sleep. After a week of that I felt well enough to reclaim my car from the Chatswood police compound. The cops were barely civil, compliant rather than cooperative. My profession still wasn't popular with the custodians of the law. They slapped me with a towing charge, a fee for holding the vehicle, and an unroadworthy notice. With the taxi fare from Glebe, it was turning out to be an expensive morning. They gave me the notice before I saw the car.

"What's this?" I said.

"Can read, can't you?" the senior constable said. "One bald tire, defective wiper, broken taillight."

"How can you tell the wiper's defective unless you turn on the ignition? And the taillight wasn't broken when I left it."

"On your way, Mr. Hardy," the senior said. "And don't get stopped between here and home with the vehicle in that condition."

"No wonder you're so popular," I said.

"Just be sure the checks you write to the Police Department and the Road Traffic Authority don't bounce."

I let him feel like a winner as he scratched his second chin. The Falcon's engine purred immediately into life, and the wipers worked fine. "Like being with the cops, do you?" I said. "Be careful or I'll trade you in."

More out of curiosity than anything else, I drove to Lindfield. The For Sale sign had been taken down, and work had been done in the garden. New owners were putting their stamp on the place. A Mitsubishi Colt was parked in the driveway, and a security screen had been installed across the front door. I wondered who had bought the house, who had got the money, and what had happened to the broken easel and the paintings. On past experience, Climpson & Carter was unlikely to enlighten me.

The drive back to Glebe didn't faze me. I found I could put my own seat belt on and everything. I celebrated by skipping the Wigram Road hike and having a couple of glasses of wine with lunch. Then I phoned Sir Phillip Wilberforce.

"Yes?" an old, cracked voice said carefully. It sounded as if he'd suddenly aged twenty years.

"Sir Phillip, this is Cliff Hardy. Do you—"

"Remember you? Of course I do. I haven't gone gaga, despite what they're trying to say. I've been hoping you'd call. We have things to talk about."

This was better than I'd hoped for. It sounded as if I were still on the payroll. "Has there been any word of your daughter?"

"Daughter," he spoke slowly, dragging the word out. "No. No. Can you come to see me?"

I said I could but I needed another day to collect something which I hoped I could find.

"You're being cryptic, your privilege, I suppose. What?"

"A photograph. I hope you can identify the subject and the photographer."

"Intriguing. Well, tomorrow then?"

"Tomorrow evening. Have you got someone looking after you?"

"Yes, damn and blast her. I'll tell her you're coming and with a bit of luck she'll let you in. Do you need any money?"

I said I didn't, and he seemed not to care one way or the other. The best kind of client. I rang off and rang Verity Lamberte's home and business numbers: no answer at the one, no information at the other, as expected. Glen had gone to Goulburn again, but before she left, she'd ascertained that the Land Cruiser was being held by the police in Katoomba and that there was no obstruction to my going and getting it. Like the good bloke he was, Terry Reeves hadn't made a peep. I rang him and told him I'd have the vehicle back tomorrow.

"No worries. How's things, Cliff?"

A question you normally answer without a thought. I couldn't do it. I said something meaningless, maybe cryptic again. Terry sounded puzzled.

* * *

The next day I caught the 8:03 to the Blue Mountains. *Rabbit at Rest* was one of the paperbacks Glen had bought me, and I was working slowly through it. It was a good book to read when you were on the right side of fifty and didn't look like dying just yet. The book held my attention, but I looked up from time to time to observe the passengers coming and going, boarding and alighting. It was good to feel like part of the moving scene again, not confined within walls. To be out there in the world where something interesting might happen. On the train nothing did, except that Rabbit's son came back from the drug rehabilitation program as a born-again Christian. Not for the first time, I was glad I hadn't had any kids.

I was in Katoomba shortly after ten. In the city it had been overcast and gloomy, but the day was clear and bright in the mountains. And cold. I'd come prepared for it in a thick shirt and heavy sweater, but the cold cut through the layers of cotton and wool, and I could feel the places where I'd been burned and lacerated stiffening. I walked up the steep main street to the police station, thinking that it was a different world up here. Sydney belonged to the ocean; the mountains belonged to the enormous country behind them. Dangerous thoughts, these, they tend to make you feel that human beings have no place on the continent at all.

The reception I got from the Katoomba cops couldn't have been more different from that in Sydney. Here I was something of a hero—the man who'd dragged the woman from the inferno and might have saved her life if help had arrived in time. No fault of his. Some city cops had been up, asking around and making themselves unpopular. Nobody gave a shit about the Loggins and Brewster case up here. There was no question of charges for bringing the Cruiser in or housing it. They told me they'd started it up every few days or so and that it was running fine. I thanked them, produced my ID, accepted their good wishes for my recovery from my injuries, and that was virtually that. I started the Cruiser and drove it out of the police car park.

A hundred yards down the road I pulled over to the curb. I got out and opened the back of the truck. There were all the things I had hastily thrown together that morning four weeks ago: the bedroll, sleeping bag, thermos. There was no sign of the leather jacket. I was sure I'd left it in the back. I yanked open the back door and looked on the seat. The newspaper I'd bought was there, along with the binoculars, which must have been taken from where I'd been observing the house. They were back in their case, safely tucked away. No whiskey, that'd have been too much to ask, but where was the jacket? I swore and searched again, but it wasn't in the Land Cruiser.

I sat behind the wheel while the light morning traffic crawled past. Nobody seemed to be in a hurry. I'd been feeling fine when I'd arrived in Katoomba; now I didn't feel so good. The morning sun coming through the windshield made me hot inside my sweater, but I'd been warned against sudden changes in temperature, so I didn't take it off. I sat, sweated, and swore. I'd been warned about getting emotionally upset, too, but I kept on swearing. *You nearly died and were on drugs for a couple of weeks*, I thought. *That could have screwed up your memory*. I tried to recall in detail my actions before I'd gone up the rock pile and I found that I couldn't.

I started the motor and headed toward Mount Victoria. The weather changed abruptly the way it can in the mountains. Some cloud came over and some mist came down, a heavy mist, needing an occasional swipe from the windshield wipers. Not ideal conditions for searching for something brown in a couple of hundred acres of bush. I took the back way in and bumped along the tracks until I found where I'd parked before going up to watch the house. This was the right place, surely—right rocks, right trees. I convinced myself and got out to search. The mist was almost a drizzle. I grabbed the groundsheet from among the camping gear and draped it over my head.

There had been a fair bit of rain up there, and the ground was slushy. Things started to come back to me as I probed around. I'd worn the jacket into town, but I'd put the parka on when I got back here because I'd thought I might have a long, cold wait up on the rocks. I'd got the binoculars and the whiskey from the seat, put them on the ground, and taken off the jacket. Then . . . I remembered. I'd slung the jacket up onto the top of the Cruiser, intending to put it away safely. And something had broken the chain of thought. It came back to me: a train whistle from the track across the valley, a long, clear sound that had cut through the chill morning air.

When had they found the Cruiser? I didn't know. If it had been late in the day, they might not have seen the jacket and just checked the vehicle over before driving off. In which direction? I searched both ways on both sides of the track for about twenty minutes before I found it. An overhanging branch must have brushed it off the roof. The jacket had fallen into a bush and lay, scarcely disturbed from the way I'd folded it, in a natural leafy shelter. It was wet and slimy, and a white mildew had formed around the seams. I stood under a tree, water dripping from the groundsheet and felt the jacket. The photograph was still there, not as crisp as before, but still there.

I ran back to the Cruiser, put the jacket on the seat beside *Rabbit at Rest*, and got moving. I needed the wipers now and the heater. My hands and feet had become cold during the search, and aches and pains had started up in various places. The warm air circulated around me, and I took a few experimental deep breaths. No wheezing, chest clear. It was some minutes before I realized that I'd turned onto the Electricity Commission service track automatically and was now heading for Salisbury Road. I had an impulse to turn around and go back the way I'd come, difficult though the maneuver would be on the narrow road. I've never understood old soldiers' desires to visit the battlefields where they'd fought and bled. I never wanted to see mine in Malaya ever again, and I felt the same about the Lambertes' cabin.

But I kept going and there it was: a collection of blackened foundation pillars, a chimney and fireplace, and a set of stone steps that led nowhere at all. The fire had consumed everything combustible. The iron roof had collapsed and lay in a jumbled heap where people had once sat and talked, ate and drunk, and made love. I stopped and looked at the ruin through the streaming windshield and the slapping wiper blades. The barbecue and water tank were intact; the burned-out 4WD had been removed. Trees on all sides of the house were charred, and heavy wheels had churned the ground into a sea of blackened mud. I had a mental flash of the woman gyrating in terror in her high-heeled shoes and erotic underwear, and of Patrick Lamberte, big and commanding in his country squire's outfit, lightly tossing the package he'd picked up at the post office. He had looked like a man turning over his cards, confidently expecting an ace. Unaccountably it was the image of the man that was most disturbing. Although by now I was warm and relatively dry inside the Cruiser, I shivered. I engaged the gear and drove fast down Salisbury Road, away from the death and destruction.

I drove straight through Mount Victoria and down to Katoomba before I felt like stopping. The visibility was bad, the road was slick, and it took all my concentration to make the run safely. Good. I was in no fit state for letting my mind drift to other matters, to faces and movements and all the other half-collected impressions. Through my association with Helen Broadway, who read philosophy and Jungian psychology, I was aware of the ragbag of memories and intuitions that make up our unconscious understanding of the world. I resisted them, always. I preferred to deal with the concrete and known—the facts, hidden and revealed, that defined the world in which work could be done, results achieved. I had a sense that I was moving beyond that world, and it alarmed and disturbed me as such feelings always have.

I pulled into a shoppers' car park off Katoomba Street and carefully unfolded the leather jacket. I slid the photograph out of the jacket pocket and opened it as delicately as if it were a three-hundred-year-old buried treasure map. The thick paper had lain inside the nylon lining of the pocket protected by several layers of leather. It was limp but not damp, and the folded sections did not stick together. When I was sure it was intact, I refolded it and headed for the Paragon Café, which is the only eating place I know in Katoomba, apart from the pubs. I wanted to sit somewhere quiet, drink coffee, and try to sort out the disturbing images that were flitting around in my brain.

The Paragon was dark, and the lunch crowd had gone. Seeing the empty seats and booths and the tables with evidence of meals consumed reminded me that I hadn't eaten. I was suddenly hungry, and it was the first time I'd felt that way since I'd woken up in the hospital. I decided it was a good sign and ordered orange juice, a club sandwich, apple pie, and a pot of coffee. I downed the orange juice in a couple of gulps and lowered the plunger in the coffeepot. Good coffee. Two sips and I unfolded the picture again and spread it out on the table.

I had never studied the photograph carefully, and what I was looking at now was very different from my memory of it. The face was clearer, and the features were more distinct. Whereas before it had seemed otherworldly, a shot taken through a screen of some kind, now it looked lifelike and immediate. Perhaps that was because I was in no doubt as to who was the subject of the picture. Unmistakable. Same incipient widow's peak, strong chin, deep-set eyes. I was looking at a photograph of the late Mr. Patrick Lamberte.

12

THE WAITRESS PUT A PLATE ON THE TABLE IN
front of me. She didn't glance at the photograph.
I didn't look at the sandwich. This was what had
been niggling at me—the as-yet-uncoded knowledge that Lamberte was the subject of the photograph. I poured out the last of the coffee. It
was cool, but I sipped it anyway as questions
flooded my brain. Who was the photographer?
Where and when was the picture taken? I'd been
half assuming, without any evidence, that Paula
Wilberforce herself was both painter and photog-

rapher. If so, what connection was there between her and Lamberte? And if not . . . Suddenly the photograph assumed greater importance. Now it was not only a possible clue to Paula Wilberforce's whereabouts but evidence of a deep hostility toward Lamberte. And therefore a lead to his murderer.

"Are you all right, sir?" The waitress was back, looking concerned.

I'd been sitting with the coffee cup in my hand, not drinking, and staring into space. I looked now at the big, bursting open sandwich— fresh lettuce, Swiss cheese, ham . . . The sight of it made me feel ill, but I forced myself to smile, take a bite, and nod appreciatively.

"Woolgathering," I said, through a mouthful.

She was in her early twenties and had probably never heard the expression. Why would anyone gather wool with several million unsalable bales sitting in the warehouses? She went away, despairing of her tip, convinced that I was insane. I munched on the sandwich without appetite. Maybe I was wrong. There are lots of men with strong chins, brown hair, and widow's peaks. John McEnroe, for example. William Hurt. And maybe the photographer had been annoyed at the execution of the shot, not the subject. I looked at the picture again and knew I was kidding myself. It *was* Patrick Lamberte, and the portraitist had hated him.

I left a good tip and most of the sandwich. The Paragon is famous for its handmade chocolates. On impulse, I bought a couple of dollars' worth of a mixed selection. I had a feeling that Terry Reeves's Wanda would be brave enough to eat liqueur-centered milk chocolates. I was pretty brave myself. I went to the nearest pub and had a couple of scotches. I hoped the whiskey might stimulate thought as well as brace me for the drive back to Sydney. Instead, I fell into a mood of self-reproach. I'd screwed up the Lamberte case from start to finish, and so far Paula Wilberforce had taken all the points. I should have checked everybody involved more carefully before I started haring off in all directions. I finished the second drink. There was a self-breathalyzer in the bar, and I dropped a dollar in it and blew in the straw. The reading was orange for caution. I swore and walked briskly back to the car. The cold air did me good and triggered some professional responses at last. When it came to checking people out, it was never too late.

* * *

On the drive back to Sydney I decided I liked the 4WD. I liked the way it held the road and the feeling of security, of being able to take the knocks. I liked the heater; I would probably get to like the cassette player. I already liked the mobile phone. I stopped in Wentworth Falls and set the machine on "broadcast." Terry Reeves was at his desk as I'd expected, and I asked him if I could hang on to the Land Cruiser for a bit.

"You sound better," he said. "Amazing what a good vehicle will do for a man."

"You can bill me for it."

"Don't worry, I will. The phone calls and everything. That's if you're working. If you're planning a holiday, I guess I can work something out."

Paula Wilberforce knows the Falcon, I thought, *but she doesn't know this crate. This is a justified expense.* "I've got a client," I said. "Thanks, Terry. Love to Wanda. I'll be in touch."

"You've got the equipment."

My next call was to Roberta Landy-Drake in Vaucluse. A sometime client, Roberta has an inexhaustible knowledge of Sydney society and its workings—at the top end. She said she'd be de-

lighted to see me. No one can say "delighted"
quite like Roberta. She was in the garden when I
pulled up outside the massive double front gates
later that afternoon. I touched the horn, and it let
out a deep bellow. Roberta lifted her head from
what she was doing and gazed calmly at the gate.
I got out and waved. She was thirty yards away
with another thirty yards to the front of the
house—a long sandstone structure that seemed
to have grown out of the earth, bringing up lawns
and trees and garden beds with it. Roberta returned my wave, reached into her gardening basket, removed something, and pointed it in my
direction. The gates slid apart like two lovers
who had done all they were going to do for now.

I drove up the gravel drive and stopped near
the rose bed where Roberta was working. She
wore a straw hat, a white silk shirt, tight trousers,
and black spike heels. Only Roberta would wear
heels to prune roses.

"Cliff," she said. "That truck thing is so very
you. So masculine. How are you, darling?"

She advanced toward me, arms outstretched,
the basket hanging from the right wrist. Roberta
is tall, thin, and very strong from all the exercise
she does to stay looking forty-five when she is
actually ten years older. Dark auburn-tinted hair

and expert makeup help the illusion. She wrapped the left arm around me and held on too hard to a burned spot. I tried not to flinch, but she felt the movement. She kissed my cheek. "What's wrong, darling? Are you hurt?"

"I was. I'm okay now. You're looking as good as ever, Roberta."

"It's a struggle," she said. A spot of rain fell, and she looked up at the gray sky. "Thank Christ. Now I can get out of this bloody garden. Come inside, you poor wounded man, and tell Roberta your troubles."

We went up the drive to the massive porch that ran the breadth of the house—a sixty-yard sandstone dash. Roberta dropped the basket with its secateurs, meager rose clippings, and remote control gate opener on the top step and marched into the house. Roberta's house has at least two rooms for every kind of activity you can think of and, for some things, five or six. She threatened to sue a magazine that said she lived alone, insisting that she lived with six other people who happened to be her servants. It was typical of Roberta that she forced the magazine to publish their names and photographs in the retraction. She was the only filthy rich person I'd ever really liked and, as far as I know, the only person in that category who ever liked me.

We went into a room where there were books, a TV set and CD player, comfortable leather chairs, and a bar.

"What do men who drive those sorts of cars drink?"

"Beer," I said.

She flicked open the fridge. "Light or . . . dark, is that what it's called?"

I laughed. "Let me get it, Roberta. You'll have . . . ?"

She glanced at the tiny diamond-studded watch on her wrist. "Low-calorie tonic with lemon and ice, fuck it."

Roberta has trouble swearing with fluency. I made her drink, opened a twist top of Cooper's Light, and sat opposite her in one of the thousand-dollar leather chairs.

"Wilberforce," I said. "What can you tell me?"

"Phillip? Oh, yes, I've heard about what happened to him. Tragic. A wonderful man. I once almost . . . but that's no great distinction."

"What d'you mean?"

"No woman under sixty was safe, darling. He must have been married at least three times, and you could multiply that by ten, if you see what I mean."

"I'm interested in the wives and children. Particularly Paula. Now, she was the daughter of . . ."

Roberta sipped her drink and settled back to enjoy herself thoroughly. Two of her husbands had been industrialists, and the other was a banker. Like the man we were speaking about, she had been an active sexual player in the social stakes where information is the basic currency. "Nancy Barlow. Bit of a mouse as I recall. Not up to Phillip's standard at all."

"Or her daughter's?"

"Dreadful child. Ran them ragged, positively ragged." Roberta smiled, showing her fine white teeth. "A bit like me when I was young, actually."

"I'll come back to her. I want to hear it all. For now, other wives, other kids?"

"Darling heart, you're asking rather a lot. Let me see. There was Lyndall Crosbie. She was an Abercrombie before she married Alistair Crosbie, the pharmaceuticals man. She had two brats by him but none, I think, by Phillip. Whatever are you doing?"

"I'm making notes. This is important. What were the names of the children?"

Roberta's high forehead wrinkled as much as she would allow it to. "Robert Crosbie and . . . Nadia."

"You're amazing. Go on."

"Phillip was married to Selina Livermore about the same time as to Nancy. A bit after, I think. Scandalously soon. I think there might have been a suggestion of bigamy, actually."

"Children?"

"You haven't touched your beer. This *must* be exciting, though I can't quite see how. Now, there was Clara, no, Karen. Awful name. Sounds like someone who might work in a nightclub selling cigarettes, don't you think?"

Roberta crossed her long, slim legs, which were still good enough to sell cigarettes, as she very well knew. She plucked the piece of lemon from her glass and sucked on it. "Cliff, why are you looking at me like that? I can't help it if all these people were playing musical chairs and swapping children backwards and forwards."

"More on Karen's mum, Selina," I said quietly. Roberta had pronounced the name Kah-ren, which I couldn't bring myself to do. "Any previous or subsequent issue?"

"I *love* legal language. It's made me so much money over the years. Yes, I'm sure there was. A girl again, by Livermore, the husband before Phillip. Poor Phillip always seemed to have females around him, like a pasha."

"Her name, Roberta, if you please."

Roberta sighed and looked around the room for inspiration. Nothing she saw helped, and she moved her head to look out the window at the water far below. The harbor was dark under the sullen sky. Roberta's finely plucked brows drew in, and a minute line appeared between them. Then she laughed and clicked her fingers. "Verity," she said. "That's it, Verity. I believe Verity and Karen hyphenated themselves for a time— Livermore-Wilberforce, if you please. Verity married that dreadful Patrick Lamberte."

"Paula Wilberforce is a stepsister to Verity Lamberte and Karen Livermore?"

"Yes. I believe Patrick's lost all his money."

I stared at her. "Paula Wilberforce, Verity and Karen Livermore-Wilberforce," I said. "Nadia and Robert Crosbie. Jesus, this is complicated."

"Are you looking for a wife, Cliff? I can find you one ever so much more suitable than any of them."

I picked up the beer and drank it in a couple

of long swallows. I'd been probing for something about Paula, some incident or association that might explain why she acted the way she did or predict what she might do next. Instead, I'd come up with a firmer connection between the two cases. It threw me. I sat in the leather chair as the light faded in the big window. Roberta looked at her watch again, clicked her tongue, and went over to the bar. She made herself a big gin and tonic and sat down with it contentedly.

"Will you please stop staring out the window. It's not at all amusing, darling. Now, d'you want to scribble down all this dirt or not?"

I forced myself to pay attention and take notes as she talked in between sips of her drink. I heard about the likelihood that Phillip Wilberforce had briefly been a bigamist and about the hippie stepdaughter Nadia, who'd run away to save a Queensland rain forest and had ended up in jail for drug smuggling.

"Only for a little while," Roberta said. "Phillip got her out quick smart. You could do things like that up there in those days, I understand."

"Right," I said. "I'm still trying to make sense of it. Paula has two stepsisters, Nadia and Verity, and one stepbrother, Robert. Also one half sister, Karen."

"Just so. That is, if the scuttlebutt is right."

"Scuttlebutt?"

"You're hopeless." She got up and walked over to where I was sitting. She took the notebook and pen from me and sketched in a family tree, pairing Phillip Wilberforce up with his wives. She drew a straight line to Paula and a wavy one to Karen. "It was said by certain malicious tongues that Phillip was the father of Karen although Selina was married to someone else at the time. Not a long marriage, I might add. Possibly of convenience, hmm?"

"Go on."

Roberta dropped the notebook into my lap and went back to her chair. "Do you know, darling," she said, "I get the distinct feeling that you've lost the thread. I thought you wanted all the goss. And there's lots more, believe me. Phillip is a most interesting man. Have you noticed how interesting people tend to attract interesting people around them? Natural, I suppose."

Roberta's notoriously weak head has been the saving of her face, figure, and brain cells. She was toward the bottom of a single stiffish gin and she was well away. She waved her glass jauntily. "You, for example. How's the delicious Helen Broadway?"

The name, with all the old pleasurable and painful associations it carried, jerked me out of my daze. "I haven't seen her for a couple of years."

"Oh, I'm sorry. Who is it now?"

"A policewoman."

"Cliff, I'm disappointed. But I must meet her. Does she have flat feet and a flat chest?" Roberta giggled and pushed out her own shapely, high-slung bosom.

I felt myself responding to what Roberta was putting out, a highly charged essence of need and desire. We had never touched except in a stylized, playacting kind of way: she the gushing socialite; I, the strong, silent pleb. I dropped my notebook and stood. She stretched in the leather chair, a slim, lithe figure. Her black trousers were tight across her flat belly and crotch. I bent over her, and she hooked an arm up around my neck. We kissed, and I could taste the gin and smell her perfume and the other womanly smells that are a part of it. Her hot tongue pushed into my mouth. I sucked on it and closed my hand around the hard mound of her right breast. She thrust up at me, giving me her mouth and her breast and wanting me to take everything else. I wanted to take it.

I pulled her to her feet. One of her shoes fell off, and she propped up awkwardly balanced, pressing into me. I was gasping for breath, and so was she. We broke the kiss, and our hands moved urgently. Then she brought her hands down sharply in fists, knocking my hands away from her body. She stepped back.

"No," she said.

"Roberta. I—"

"We're friends."

I reached for her. "We can still be friends."

The banality of what I said cut through the lust and confusion. We both laughed. I struggled to recapture the moment. I got close to her and cupped my hands around her firm buttocks, pulling her toward me. She was rigid with resistance. Her legs were locked together. I released her and moved back.

"Cliff, I'm sorry."

"It's okay," I said. I cleared my throat, fighting to get out of the rutting mood, fighting off disappointment and anger. "You're probably right."

She flopped down into her seat. She looked as exhausted as I felt. "Did you ever go to bed with that lodger of yours, Hildegarde?"

"No."

"Isn't she still a friend?"

"She's married to Frank Parker. They have a son named Cliff."

We sat in our respective chairs, both silent. A snatch of doggerel ran through my head:

Higamous, hogamous, women are monogamous,
Hogamous, higamous, men are polygamous.

Right, I thought. *Women are smarter.* Like a lot of men, maybe most, I'd dreamed of attaining a perfect polygamy, a different woman for different situations and moods. Experience had taught me that it was a difficult condition to organize and an impossible one to sustain. Most of the women I'd had anything to do with seemed to know that instinctively. Even Helen Broadway, who'd let it run to the sixth tackle, had known in her heart that it couldn't work.

"Cliff?"

I'd left her adrift in her own thoughts, memories, and regrets. I forced a grin and picked up my notebook. "Tell me everything you can about Paula Wilberforce."

Roberta's finely sculptured face lost its bruised look and its tension. "Dogs," she said. "Mad about dogs. Can't understand it myself, darling. I was terribly keen on horses."

13

THE WOMAN WHO OPENED THE DOOR OF
Phillip Wilberforce's house was about the same
age as Roberta Landy-Drake, but she hadn't
made a career out of looking younger. She was of
medium height and plump. She wore her gray
hair short and very little makeup. Her dress was
a plain blue worn with a heavy white cardigan. A
pair of spectacles hung on a light cord around her
neck. She looked intelligent and capable.

"My name's Hardy," I said.

"I'm Pamela Darcy. Please come in, Mr. Hardy. He's expecting you."

That got us off on the right foot as far as I was concerned. I was relieved that she hadn't said, "Sir Phillip," the way some people working for titled employers do when they want some of the gilt to rub off on them.

"How is he, Mrs. Darcy?"

"Not strong, but fighting. He's got a touch of lung trouble, which is worrying at his age. I'd ask you not to tire him and so on, but I know it'd be a waste of time."

We were climbing the stairs. "How's that?" I said.

"He'll do exactly as he pleases."

We stopped outside the master bedroom. Mrs. Darcy knocked firmly and walked straight in. I got the impression that an interesting battle of two strong wills was going on here. The old man was sitting up propped on a heap of pillow in the big bed. His tan had faded to a sallowness, and his hair lay flat on his skull. He looked like an old China hand who'd spent so long in the East he'd taken on an Oriental appearance. This was emphasized by the embroidered silk dressing gown he wore over a black pajama top. Gold-framed half glasses balanced on his nose.

"A decent pause before entering is customary, Mrs. Darcy," Wilberforce growled. "What if I'd been doing something you wouldn't like to see?"

"It's hardly appropriate for you to invoke what is customary," Mrs. Darcy said. "Have you taken your medicine?"

"Damn you, yes."

"Damn you too. Would you like a drink, Mr. Hardy?"

"Of course he would," Wilberforce said. "And get one for me while you're at it. Scotch, Hardy?"

"That'd be fine."

I sat down in a chair that, as I recalled, had served for Wilberforce to throw clothes over. Now the room was tidy but not fussy. A coat hung on the back of the door, there were books and magazines on the bed and bedside table, and the several bottles of pills, glass, and water jug hadn't been neatly arranged.

Wilberforce snorted as he saw me taking in the details. "She wanted to put flowers in here, but I wouldn't allow it. I told her flowers remind me of death."

"I prefer them outside myself," I said. "Otherwise, how's she treating you?"

"She's worth talking to. What's that you've got there?"

I was unfolding the photograph. The intense interest in his voice suggested that he lacked stimulation. I hoped I wasn't going to give him too much. I leaned forward and put the picture in front of him. He pushed his glasses up into position.

"Huh, out of focus. Typical."

"Have you ever seen it before? Do you know who took it?"

Mrs. Darcy came in and handed me a solid scotch in a heavy glass. The glass she gave her patient contained about half as much. I refused water. She poured a generous amount into his over his protest.

"Drowning good whiskey. My grandfather would have had you shot for that."

Mrs. Darcy was a last-word specialist. "And your great-great-grandfather would have turned in his grave." She smiled at me and left the room.

"That Wilberforce," I said. "Freed the slaves?"

"Silly old fool didn't live to see it. Died a month too soon." He sipped his whiskey and made a face. "It's always too soon. Now this photograph, it could be one of Paula's. Where did you get it?"

"From the house in Lindfield. Is she a painter as well?"

"Yes. Competent, no more." He sounded indifferent, even dismissive, but he let his fingers rest on the surface of the photograph. "What're these shapes in the background?"

The overhead light falling on the picture highlighted several vague forms behind the subject in the foreground. I hadn't seen them before. Interesting, but not as interesting as the next question I had to ask.

"Do you recognize the face?"

He adjusted his glasses and peered more closely. "No. She's taken a brush to it by the looks. Well, that's Paula. Who is it?"

"I believe it's Patrick Lamberte."

"Oh, stepdaughter's husband. Funny chap. Yes, it could be. Odd, though."

He doesn't know they're dead, I thought. I took refuge in my drink. It was good whiskey. "Why odd?"

"Paula and Verity hated each other on sight as children. Wouldn't have thought they'd had any contact as adults." He drank again and appeared to be listening to a replay of his words inside his head. "Trouble, Hardy? More trouble?"

"I'm afraid so."

I told him what had happened at Mount Victoria, giving it to him as gently as I could. He nodded as he listened, sighed, and occasionally shook his head. Our drinks were empty by the time I'd finished. My throat was dry, and the old man was quietly weeping.

"Karen," he said huskily. "Selina's girl. Selina said she was mine, and she may have been. Certainly the resemblance was there. But you know, I was so busy in those days I can hardly remember her. Those poor, poor children. I made a terrible mess of things."

"There were mothers and other fathers involved. You don't have to take all the blame."

"I have to take it for Paula. I spoiled her, indulged her in every way, but I didn't take the trouble to find out what she was really like until it was too late."

"I have to find her. Not only for your sake, for hers and mine." I told him that it was my gun that he had been shot with and that Paula might have another round still in it.

"She knows nothing about firearms so far as

I'm aware," he said. "That's extremely dangerous."

"This is painful for you, but can you tell me
what she said to you that day?"

He closed his eyes and sighed. With his damp
cheeks and bloodless lips he looked dead, and I
wouldn't have been surprised to have heard the
rattle. But he roused himself, struggled up
against the pillows, and handed me his glass.
"Go down and get us both a refill, will you, old
chap?"

"What will Mrs. Darcy say?"

"It'll be up to you to convince her. I'm going
to sit here and collect my thoughts for a minute."

I found Mrs. Darcy sitting at the kitchen table
doing a cryptic crossword. She had pocket edi-
tions of a dictionary and a thesaurus to hand and
was arranging letters in a circle, working with a
pencil and eraser on a scribbling pad. For one
terrible moment I thought she was going to ask
me to provide a word. I can't understand the
questions in cryptic crosswords, let alone come
up with the answers. But she didn't. Instead, she
frowned at the glasses.

"Make it a very weak one," I said. "Just to jog
his memory."

"And you, are you driving, Mr. Hardy?"

"Not yet," I said.

She got a bottle of Black Douglas from a cupboard and poured one judicious and one very judicious measure into the glasses. She added the water. Then she surprised me by taking down another glass and pouring herself a solid slug.

"I won't tell," I said.

She took a sip. "Tell all you like. Are you a policeman?"

I shook my head. "A private enquiry agent. He's hired me to find his daughter."

"I see. Which one?"

"Paula."

"Ah, yes. The dog girl. Very strange."

"I'm not with you."

"Can you imagine what it's like to take care of rich people in their houses? No, how could you? Or perhaps you do. You become involved and . . . inquisitive. You have time on your hands. What do you think of him?"

I shrugged. "He's probably been a right bastard in his time, but he's paying his dues now. Despite myself, I quite like him."

"So do I. You seem to be a decent man, and I know he's worried about Paula. He's had a stroke, and I doubt if his memory is up to much. Ask him about Paula's photographs."

"That's already come up."

She nodded and sipped her whiskey. Her eyes drifted to the crossword, and she stabbed at a word on the scribbling pad with her pencil. "Ah. Good! See me when you've finished, Mr. Hardy."

The old man had slumped down on the bed, and his eyes were closed again. His face was dry now, but there was a lost, defeated look about him. He heard me coming, and his old, wrinkled eyelids lifted. "Did she give you the drinks?"

"Yes." I handed it across, and he took a sip. It didn't seem to interest him.

"I've been trying, but I simply can't remember anything useful about anything. It's like living in the clouds. I have memories, but they're oddly detached from each other. There's no sequence and no clarity. I can remember things that have been said to me, but not who said them. I can recall places but not who I was with. It's a terrible thing to lose your life in this way, Hardy. It makes what's left seem not worth having."

"Maybe you can get it back."

He shook his head. "Doubt it. Doubt if I can be bothered."

This was bad news for yours truly. I sat down

and sipped my scotch, waiting for him to give me the boot—if he could be bothered. The whiskey seemed to perk him up, though. A little color came back into his face, and he set his jaw in what must have been a very determined jut in his younger days. "But I want to see Paula again. I want to make my peace with her."

"I asked you what she said before she shot you."

"Buggered if I can remember. If it comes back to me, I'll let you know. Meanwhile, what will you do?"

"There's some sort of connection between Paula and Verity. I'll look for them both. There's ways: parking fines, credit card checks, people to talk to. I hadn't even started when all this happened."

He nodded and lifted his free hand from the bedcovers like a benediction. "Do what you have to. Need more money?"

"Not yet."

"Verity and Paula. Can't understand it. Hated each other on sight . . ."

His voice was fading, and the glass in his hand drooped. Whiskey and water slopped into the bed. I took the glass and put it on the bedside table.

"I believe there's a collection of Paula's photographs in the house. I'd like to take a look at them. Maybe take a couple away."

"Yes," he said. A spark of memory flared. "Verity killed a dog."

"What?"

"She killed a dog and Paula . . ."

"Did what?"

He shook his head. The clouds had come down again, enveloping and confusing him. I took Paula's photograph of Lamberte from the bed and went away quietly, carrying my drink and hoping very strongly I'd be able to give him what he wanted.

Mrs. Darcy was waiting for me at the foot of the stairs.

"He's asleep," I said. "Or very close to it. I mentioned the photographs. He said it was okay for me to take any I needed."

She pointed through the archway into the sitting room and went up the stairs. I took a drink and moved in the direction she'd indicated. There was a deep, fresh scar plowed into the parquet floor, and one of the cabinets was missing a glass panel—evidence of Paula's visit.

Three fat, bulging photograph albums were sitting on a coffee table. I opened one and read the childishly formed handwriting: "Paula Wilberforce, her pictures." The second album had "P. WILBERFORCE" printed in severe block capitals on the inside cover. The third had no identification at all.

I was too tired to start leafing through them now, too tired to be likely to notice what was significant and what wasn't. I went to the stairs and listened, but I couldn't hear anything. I finished my drink and took the glass out to the kitchen. Mrs. Darcy had wrapped up the crossword. It lay there with every square neatly filled in. I looked at it and thought about the comparison it presented to the shambles of the Wilberforce-Lamberte case. What sort of case was it? Missing persons? Attempted murder? An actual double murder? Sororicide? Was there such a crime?

I was past coherent thought. I rinsed the glass and put it on the sink. I needed to stay in Mrs. Darcy's good books. Then I collected the photograph albums and let myself out of the house. It loomed up above me, dark on the top story apart from one light in the master bedroom. I tramped down the path toward the gate. The albums weighed a ton. My back hurt; the whiskey was acidic in my empty stomach, and the arousal I'd felt back at Roberta's was a distant, shameful memory. I pushed open the gate and headed for the solid, comforting shape of the Land Cruiser.

A man stepped from behind the vehicle, a big man, moving close. He said, "Hardy?" and put his hand in his pocket.

I had too much frustration, doubt, and worry built up inside me to react other than violently. I dropped the photograph albums and hit him in the ribs with a punch that sent waves of pain through my back and shoulders but still felt good. He bellowed and threw a fast punch at my face, but I stepped inside it and banged him again in the same spot. He was strong; he grunted and tried to kick me. A mistake, always a mistake. He was off-balance when I caught him with a solid right jolt to the side of the jaw. His knees wobbled, and he sagged toward the Land Cruiser. I moved forward; it was like being back in the Police Boys Club in a three-rounder with the opponent tired and on the ropes. I felt young and strong again, and I measured him for a combination.

"Don't hit him again. Don't!"

The woman's voice was close, almost in my ear. I kept an eye on my man, but the moment had passed. He lifted his hands protectively and Verity Lamberte stepped between us.

14

SHE HAD LOST MOST OF THE SMARTNESS AND
dash she'd displayed when she'd come to my office. How long ago was it? It seemed like
months. She was thinner, her hair was lank, and
in trousers, sweater, and padded jacket she
looked drab. But it was still her. Instinctively I
reached out to grab her arm and stop her from
running. But she stood there with no thought of
flight. The man pulled out a handkerchief and
wiped blood from his face. My punch had caused
his nose to bleed.

"Mr. Hardy," Verity Lamberte said.

"The same." I gestured toward the man. "Who's this?"

"My stepbrother, Robert. We—we just wanted to talk."

"To talk," Robert said.

On closer inspection, he wasn't so big. Only a fraction taller than I was, and some of the bulk was in his clothes. Still, he'd made some pretty good moves. He was pale-faced and a touch weak-chinned. I was relieved to see that he wasn't wearing glasses.

"Talk is right," I said. "What the hell's going on here? Where have you been?"

"Hiding. With Robert."

"Great. And what're you doing here? Don't tell me you've followed me all day like your crazy sister did. I couldn't stand it."

She stared at me uncomprehendingly. "Karen followed you?"

"Not Karen, Paula."

"She's not . . . I haven't seen *her* for years."

Robert put his handkerchief away. His eyes drifted to the albums lying on the nature strip. "We came to see him." He pointed at the Wilberforce mansion. "We thought he might be able to help."

"You can't see him now. He's asleep."

"Maybe you can help me," Verity said.

Robert shook his head. "I don't think that's such a good idea."

"I think it's a great idea," I said. I was still holding her arm. I released her and bent to pick up the albums. When I had them under my arm, I took hold of her again. "Where can we go to talk?"

I drove with Verity in the Land Cruiser, following Robert in his Audi. Our talking place proved to be Robert Crosbie's three-bedroom flat in Bellevue Hill. Robert turned out to be a computer programmer and electrical engineer who'd inherited money from about three different directions the way the rich do. He was a bachelor, running his own small business and very attached to his stepsister, Verity. She had been staying with him since the visit from the police to tell her of her husband's death. Verity's mother, who was Selina Livermore before she became Wilberforce (she was subsequently Ashley-Hawkins, I was told), was keeping an eye on the two children. They had temporarily become boarders at their respective private schools, which they found a great lark.

"I *loved* being a boarder," Verity said.

Robert nodded.

I had nothing to contribute at this point, having walked to Maroubra High for five years from our semi. All this information had poured out almost as soon as we entered the flat. Stepbrother and stepsister were dead keen to show how solid their family was, how caring and protective. I dumped the albums on the living room table and asked if there was anything to eat. The half sandwich consumed in Katoomba seemed like an experience from another lifetime.

Robert said, "Sure, sure," and went off to busy himself in his bachelor kitchen.

Verity and I sat in armchairs a yard apart. Although her looks had suffered, for a woman who had lost a husband and a sister and whose kids were on hold, she was bearing up pretty well. I thought she could take some direct action. I said, "Did you know he was screwing Karen?"

She shook her head. "No. But she was very attractive."

"Right," I said. "I saw her in all her fucking togs. Trouble was . . . her hair was on fire."

She closed her eyes. "Do you have to be offensive?"

"Widow Lamberte," I said, "I went into that house when it was going up like a bonfire. I got Karen out, but she was too badly burned and smoke-affected to live. I nearly died myself. The cops very naturally wanted to know what I was doing up there with my binoculars and survival gear. I told them, but you weren't around to back up my story."

"I was afraid. The police came and told me there'd been a fire and that Patrick was dead. They didn't mention you. But I thought . . . when they heard about you and the bullets and everything, they'd blame me. They'd think I killed them. You know what they do! You know how they falsely accuse people and ruin their lives."

She was right. There had been a rash of cases of just that kind lately, affecting people of all classes and walks of life. My own insecurities derived from problems within the law enforcement structure.

"I was so scared," she said. "I came to Robert and asked Mother to help. She told me about Karen when the police told her. That made me even more frightened. I tried to get in touch with you, but your phones didn't answer. I didn't know what to do, so I just hid here. Robert's the one who's held this crazy family together. The only one!"

Robert came back bearing a wooden platter with five different varieties of cheese, dry biscuits, sliced salami, black olives, and a bottle of Wolf Blass red.

"Will this do?" he said.

I ate and drank, fueling up, and didn't say anything at all for a few minutes. Robert and Verity sipped their wine and nibbled.

"Thanks," I said. "I was running on empty. D'you know who shot Phillip Wilberforce?"

Both shook their heads.

Robert said, "Verity was getting edgy about just . . . hiding. She thought he might be able to help her to deal with the police, you know? But he was in hospital for quite some time. We waited until tonight to visit. Then we saw you."

A lateral thinker.

"Who shot him?" Verity said.

I took a swig of Wolf Blass. "Paula."

Verity almost dropped her glass. "God, does that mean *she* . . ."

"What?" I said.

"Had anything to do with Patrick and Karen's deaths?"

"Big jump," I said. "You'd like that, would you?"

Robert put his glass on the table. "Hardy . . ."

"Shut up. I've been hired by your sometime stepfather to find Paula."

"That'd be right," Verity said. "She was the only fruit of his loins. The only one of us he ever cared a fuck about."

"Verity!"

"Shut up, Robert."

"Happy families," I said. "Let's look at some snaps." I opened the first of the albums. Our three heads craned forward as we examined the first page. Four photographs were carefully mounted by means of the old stickdown corners method. The pictures were of children, in twos and threes, grouped around a birthday cake. Robert pulled back sharply.

"What's the point of this?" he said.

I began to flick over the leaves as Verity gazed, rapt. "I don't know. To try to spot something that might suggest where Paula is or what she might do next."

Verity laughed. "If you really knew Paula, you wouldn't even think that."

Robert grabbed the second album. "I'll show you something. If there was anyone she wanted to kill, it was Verity. Where are they? Yes, here."

He opened the book at a double-page spread of ten photographs, all of the same subject—a dead dog.

Verity gasped. "It was an accident. I didn't mean to kill him."

"He was a nasty, vicious brute," Robert said. "The rest of us were glad you did."

The dog was a whitish bull terrier. It lay on its side with its tongue hanging out. There was a dark, gaping wound the size of a fist in its neck.

"It happened at this place in the country we used to go to. I found a shotgun in a shed. It was old and very rusty. I pointed it at Rudi, and it went off. I was terrified by the noise, and the gun hurt me when it fired. I was terrified of Paula, too. Rudi was her dog. She came running up. She grabbed the gun, and I think she would have beaten my brains in with it if someone hadn't stopped her."

"Mummy," Robert said, which, under the circumstances, wasn't very enlightening.

"Instead, she took dozens of pictures of Rudi.

She used to leave them on my bed, put them in my books. It was sickening."

"Let me get this straight," I said. "You all used to hang around together, even after the divorces and so on?"

Robert nodded. "It was horrible. *The Brady Bunch* was on TV then. Verity and Nadia and I used to look at it and laugh. Our lives weren't anything like that."

Verity turned the page. "I suppose they were trying to make some sort of family life, even though they'd screwed up their own lives. I mean Paula's father and my mother and Robert's."

"Is that what you called him—Paula's father?"

"I didn't call him anything to his face," Robert said. "I just couldn't. I never saw my own father after they divorced. It . . ."

He retreated to a chair and sat down. "God," he said. "That's why I've never married. I never wanted to put anyone through any of that. The fights they had, the savagery. It was all lawyers and courts and houses being sold."

Verity was crying now. "And kids being put in boarding school. I *hated* boarding school."

I turned over the pages of the albums, occasionally asking for an identification or a date, which one or the other of them gave me indifferently. They were both sunk in depression, induced by memories of childhood. It was sad to see, but I had work to do. Eventually I accumulated pictures of all the wives and kids. A tall dark girl with a Gypsy mane of hair was identified by Verity as Nadia.

"She's dead," Robert said. "She had an accident."

"What sort of accident?"

He thrust out his underslung chin, ready to take another unhappy memory on it. "She was washed off some rocks in Queensland. She drowned."

I grunted sympathetically and made a note. "No pictures of Paula herself. Why's that?"

"Paula never let anyone touch her camera," Verity said.

"There must have been other cameras around."

Robert shook his head. "Paula never let herself be photographed. She wouldn't even sit for the school photograph session. I remember we once tried to force her—"

"Who's we?" I said.

"Nadia and I. I tried to hold her while Nadia took the snap. Paula fought like a tiger. I couldn't hold her. She scratched Nadia's face and broke the camera. No one tried again after that."

"What was Paula's attitude to you?"

"She despised me, as she despised all men."

"What about her and Karen?"

They exchanged looks as if considering cooking up a story. Then Verity shrugged. "She and Karen got on fine. Karen was the only one of us Paula had any time for."

"It was strange," Robert said. "Karen wasn't *his* child any more than the rest of us, although Paula said she was. They looked rather alike, but Karen's mother had been such a slut anyone could've been the father. Paula called Karen her real sister, but I think it was just because she shared her liking for dogs."

I was drawing lines on the page of my notebook, connecting names. "I don't get it. You were just kids. You couldn't have known anything about . . ."

"We did!" Verity snapped. "We knew all about it. *They* never talked about anything else except who was screwing who, and who had whose nose and eyes. It was sick."

"It was baronial," Robert said. "He liked to accumulate the women and children and dogs and cats around him like a medieval baron. Actually, I think the Wilberforces ran cotton factories or something."

"Barons need acres." I tapped the photograph I'd detached of the dead dog. "This place in the country, does Wilberforce still own it?"

"Fitzroy House, near Mittagong," Verity said. "No, it was sold off sometime back in one of the divorce settlements. I'm not sure, but I don't think he's got anything left now except that ghastly place in Randwick. Randwick!"

I drank some more of the wine and felt a terminal tiredness creeping over me. Running into dead ends didn't help. I asked them if they could give me the names of any of Paula's friends. Verity cracked the first smile I'd seen from her that night.

"None," she said. "Zero."

"Come on. Her father told me she'd lived with a man for a time."

Verity shook her head. "Not in *that* way. I'd bet anything she's a virgin."

Robert blushed and plucked at the skin on a bit of salami. "I'm getting a bit sick of all this about Paula. We've spent more time thinking about her tonight than she'd have spent thinking about anyone else in her whole bloody life.

What's so important about Paula? What about Verity's problem?"

I could see his point. I told them about the gun and how Paula had used it to shoot Phillip Wilberforce. I told them that the pistol might still be loaded. They were both stunned.

"She couldn't have meant to kill him," Verity said. "Not unless she's gone completely crazy. If you kill someone, you can't inherit their estate, right?"

"As far as I know," I said. "I thought there wasn't much of an estate. Just the house."

For some reason, all the talk and drama had restored some vitality to Verity. She pushed back her hair; the wine had done something for her color, and her eyes were brighter. "D'you realize what that dreadful pile is *worth*? I remember Patrick put a valuation on it once—a couple of million."

"Not in this market," I said.

"Still, a million five, at least."

Robert seemed to find all this distasteful, or perhaps he just had good powers of concentration. "Verity, Hardy—what's she going to do?"

I rubbed my long dark stubble and felt my injured back stiffening, the skin on the burned patches growing tight. The itch in my fingers where the split skin had only just healed made me want to scratch. "Paula's psychotic, it looks like. She's got things against you both. She had something against Patrick Lamberte."

Verity snorted derisively. "She didn't! Patrick? She scarcely ever met him."

I took the defaced photograph from my pocket and spread it out on the table. "This is Paula's work. I've reason to believe that she treated a painting of Patrick in the same way."

Verity gaped at the creased, well-worn picture.

"He's naked. I can't believe it. Patrick and Paula? No."

"What're those shapes in the background?" Robert said.

"Who cares about fucking shapes in the background?" Verity screamed. "This is my husband, posing naked for that crazy bitch."

"Not necessarily," I said. "She could have airbrushed the photo, doctored it in some way. I haven't had a chance yet to find out."

Verity slumped back in her chair. "That bastard! That slut! I want a cigarette."

"You don't smoke," Robert said.

"I stopped. Now I want to start again."

Robert stopped staring at the photograph and flapped his hands uselessly. "Hardy?"

I shook my head. "Tomorrow we'll go and see your solicitor, Mrs. Lamberte. Then we'll trot along and you'll make a statement to the police. I'll support everything you say. You'll be off the hook, I'm sure. You can get to see your kids again."

Verity let go a long sigh. "Thank God."

Robert was the only one who didn't seem to think it was a brilliant strategy.

15

BRIAN GARFIELD, VERITY'S SOLICITOR, WAS a man I'd done business with before. When I showed up with Verity at his office in Neutral Bay, he controlled his surprise by expressing his agitation.

"Verity, my God, where have you been? I've had the police and the bank and every Tom, Dick, and Harry after you."

"I'm sorry, Brian. I believe you know Cliff Hardy."

I'd told Verity about my former dealings with

Garfield on the drive to Neutral Bay. I'd spent the night in Robert's spare room, used his shower, shampoo, and a disposable razor, and accepted a croissant and coffee for breakfast. I was feeling better than I had for many days. Well enough to pretend that I was happy to see Garfield again. We shook hands warily.

His offices were all blue walls, gray carpets, and white furniture. It felt like stepping into a modern art exhibition. I like the old-time legal offices where thick files tied up with pink ribbon are stuffed into bookcases and there are rows and rows of legal reports with cracked bindings. The reports were there all right, but the bindings looked as though they'd never been bent. I knew where all the files were—on computer discs. Garfield ordered coffee for us from a secretary in a tight skirt, and we settled down, him behind his big, empty desk and Verity and I in sweetly padded chairs.

"Tragic business, my dear," Garfield said. "I hope . . ."

Verity had cleaned herself up. She shone again, if not quite with the same luster as before, then with enough to suggest she'd get it all back in time. "I didn't do it, Brian," she said brightly.

Garfield undid the buttons on his double-breasted suit jacket. There were quite a lot of buttons. He was a small man with a big ego. I am a biggish man with an ego smaller than his. His size had something to do with his ego. I had worked for him on a white-collar crime case which he'd lost. We had not got on well.

"Of course you didn't. Ah, coffee."

He made a fuss over the coffee and drew the whole business out for twice the necessary length. I recalled that he charged by the hour.

"I want to make a statement to the police. Mr. Hardy has already made a statement. He wishes to add a few things in support of mine."

"I see. No problem."

"Detective Sergeant Willis is the man to get hold of," I said.

Garfield stabbed a button on his console and asked someone to get him Willis on the phone. Maybe it was the same woman who'd made the coffee. If so, she was scoring well that morning. Garfield was talking to Willis within thirty seconds. The lawyer didn't say much. Verity drank her coffee and looked serene. I drank mine and felt uneasy. I was uneasy about her serenity, but what do I know about widowhood and parenthood? I began to wonder whether Verity would inherit anything from Patrick besides bad memories. Would Brian know? It didn't matter because he wouldn't tell me. Still, it was something to think about instead of gray carpet and blue walls.

Garfield replaced the phone. "He can see us in an hour."

"Good," Verity said. "How does Patrick's death affect the Family Court proceedings?"

Garfield looked at his watch. "Renders them null and void. Of course, many loose ends to tie up. But your worries about getting sole custody are . . . as things have turned out, at an end."

If you leave matters to people like Garfield, they'll smooth everything over at a hundred dollars an hour no matter how long it takes. I put my coffee cup and saucer down on his white desk awkwardly, so that some of the coffee slopped out onto the snowy surface. "How does Verity stand in relation to Patrick's estate?" I said.

Garfield was shocked, or pretended to be. "Really, Hardy. I don't . . ."

"Sure you do, Brian. The wife is suspect numero uno until someone else is nailed. Verity hired me to sniff around Patrick. She didn't ask your permission. We're both slightly in the shit, as you'll see when we meet Willis. Patrick was screwing Verity's sister."

"Some sister," Verity snarled.

"You see how it is, Brian. The Family Court may be happy with a few well-worded depositions, but the police won't be."

Garfield, to give him his due, was a fighter if sufficiently provoked. "With a roughneck like you involved, I suppose you're right. I can't imagine what possessed you to engage this man, Verity. He's . . ."

"Honest, I think. How *do* I stand in relation to Patrick's crumbling empire?"

"I don't know," Garfield muttered. "You'd have to ask Clive Stephenson, and I very much doubt that he'd tell you."

I had my notebook out. "Is that with a *v* or a *ph*, Brian?"

"Get stuffed," Garfield said.

Verity giggled. "Brian, name and address, please."

"With a *ph*. Stephenson, Bedford and Waters, Martin Place."

I scribbled, put the notebook away, and got out of my chair. "Let's go and see the cops."

Verity was good, very good. She told her story fluently, but not too fluently, with emotion, but not too much emotion. It pretty much dovetailed with what I'd said because I'd worded her up that way. I made a brief statement confirming a few things, dotting an *i* and crossing a *t* or two. This time we didn't have to wait for a printout. It came at the touch of a few keys, and Verity and I signed.

Willis escorted us out the rear exit into the dark alley which is all College Lane is and called me back. I hesitated. My business with Verity Lamberte was finished on one level; on another I was reluctant to let her walk off. We had driven to the city in the Land Cruiser. Garfield had his BMW. He offered to drive Verity to her mum's place in Point Piper. What could I say? I waved them good-bye and turned back to Willis.

"I'm surprised to see you lined up with that little prick, Hardy," Willis said.

"I'm not lined up with him."

"What about her? Cool as you like. Reckon she did it?"

"No."

Willis dug in one ear with his forefinger and examined the result. "Smith and Wesson thirty-eight automatic pistol, serial number AS one-two-three-slash-four-eight-seven-four, issue permit number . . . shit, I forget. It's not doing you any good, having that floating around."

"Tell me about it. I was hoping you'd had some sightings of Paula Wilberforce. Found her car. Something like that."

"Fuck all. Have you got anything else to tell me?"

Willis's face was a mask of nondisclosure. I took my cue from him.

"Nothing," I said.

He flicked the dirty ear wax against the door of a parked police car. "Here's something. You know a trick cyclist named Holmes?"

"I've met him."

"We got on to him. He treated the Wilberforce nutter. Wouldn't tell us a bloody thing, of course. I mentioned you and how it was your gun that did the job. You know, since everything was so confidential, like."

"Sure," I said.

"He said he'd be willing to talk to you."

"He probably only said that because he didn't like you."

"I don't give a shit." Willis moved forward quickly and jabbed my third shirt button with a blunt, hard finger. "You go and see him, Hardy. Have a cozy chat. And if you get anything useful, I want to hear it next. Understand?"

"Or else what?"

He turned away and moved back toward the door. "Or I'll have a good shot at yanking your fucking license."

I drove to St. Peters Lane and parked the Land Cruiser where I usually park the Falcon. With no sticker it was in danger of incurring a fine, but what the hell? I was already being treated like an outlaw. My office had accumulated several weeks' worth of junk mail, bills, receipts, and dust. I dealt with it all systematically, hoping that routine tasks would bring with them some clear thinking, even insights. Nothing came. As I cleared away the scraps of paper I'd used to wrap the bullets, I started to think about explosives. No one I'd met so far in this business had struck me as a mad bomber. But I realized how little I knew about most of them—particularly Karen Livermore and Lamberte. Could Patrick Lamberte have blown himself up by accident or design?

When I'd cleared the debris and written a few checks to pay overdue bills, I rang Dr. John Holmes in Woollahra. I had a clear memory of the place—a tree-shaded street with deep gardens fronting elegant Victorian houses. They were the sorts of houses that cost a fortune to buy, another fortune to restore, and a hell of a lot to maintain. A woman answered the phone. I stated my name and business and was put straight through to Holmes.

"Mr. Hardy, the private detective," he said in his honeyed tones. "I trust you are well."

"I've been better and I've been worse, Doctor. How about you?"

"Hmm, much the same I'd say. Could you come here? I'd rather like to talk to you."

"About Paula Wilberforce. Why?"

"Have you any idea how many women kill their fathers?"

"No, how many?"

"Virtually none. It's of the utmost urgency that she be located and given treatment."

"Is she dangerous?"

"Very."

Darlinghurst to Woollahra is ten minutes in time, a couple of miles in distance, and a huge leap economically and socially, but I had no reason to feel uncomfortable. As I drove along Holmes's street, I noticed that the Land Cruiser fitted in nicely. A good number of its brothers and cousins were nestled into the driveways and carports. I've been told that the great majority of

4WDs sold in Australia never leave the bitumen. They are status symbols and dream machines. "One day, Vanessa, I'll sell the agency and we'll drive around Australia. I've always wanted to see Kakadu." But Vanessa ends up driving the thing to do the shopping, while Jeffrey takes the Volvo to work.

I parked outside Holmes's high brick wall and was surprised to see the extra security systems installed since my last visit a few years back. More status trappings, maybe. The squawk box and buzzer got me through the gate but only into a tunnel that led to the front door. The tunnel was constructed of metal bars, thin but tough-looking and too closely meshed to allow escape. The bars were arched across the path, bolted into a track along the bottom and into the high side wall. Outside them the garden was lush and green, but the bars spoiled the effect.

I tramped up toward the front door and the bell. There was absolutely nothing else to do. As I stepped up onto the porch, I expected a metal grille to come slamming down behind me. Instead, I got looked at through a fish-eye lens and there was more electronic communication.

A female voice said, "Can you show some identification, please?"

I held my license folder up to the lens.

"Thank you."

The door opened, and I moved into the big entrance area that I remembered from my first visit. The huge mirror was still there, but not the woman dressed in riding gear. Now she was wearing jogging clothes—a white designer tracksuit with headband and Reeboks. The sneakers squeaked on the polished floor as she jogged gently on the spot.

"Up the stairs and the first on the right."

"Aren't you going to come?" I said. "Great for the hamstrings."

She giggled and kept on jogging.

I went up the stairs and opened the door she'd indicated. Dr. John Holmes rose from behind his desk and moved forward to meet me. He had become even more bearlike with the passage of a few years—massive chest, huge shoulders. His heavy-jowled face was dominated by a broad, spreading nose and thick pepper-and-salt eyebrows. I prepared myself for his grip but was surprised to find it mild. The other time we'd shaken he'd nearly demobilized the thumb and two fingers.

"Hardy, yes. You've been through a bit since we last met, I see. Sit down. Sit down."

He'd been through something himself. He'd gained weight, lost hair, and his eyes were muddy. One of his thin cigars was burning in an ashtray on the desk, and he picked it up and inhaled as if he wanted both lungs to be completely filled. I sat down in a chair pulled up close to the desk, well away from the leather couch. A blind had been drawn halfway down the big window behind Holmes's desk, and the room was gloomy. The smoke he was exhaling went up and floated around the ceiling rose. The hand I'd shaken, the books in the shelves on three walls, the chair, all smelled of cigar smoke.

"Paula Wilberforce," I said. "Your patient."

He inclined his head. "And to you . . . ?"

"Daughter of my client."

"Ah, yes, the egregious Sir Phillip. Do you know what that word means, Hardy?"

"I've got a rough idea. Don't patronize me, Doctor, and don't waste my time, which is as valuable to me as yours is to you, even if less well paid."

He laughed. "I'd forgotten how direct you were. I'm sorry. Do you have any idea of the damage Phillip Wilberforce has done?"

I shrugged. "I've met some of the children, stepchildren, whatever. I haven't met their mothers and teachers and friends. I don't know what they had on their DNAs."

"Quite. You're right to reprimand me. Personalities are formed multicausally, of course. But there are dominant causes, and Sir Phillip Wilberforce's example and behavior are just such things."

"Maybe," I said. "I'm inclined to think that you have to take responsibility for what you're like at some point in your life. Maybe not at eighteen, but by, let's say, thirty or so."

"If only it were that easy. Have you accepted responsibility for what you are?"

"Sure. I'm impatient, suspicious, inclined to be violent. It buggers me up sometimes, but I try not to let it bugger up other people. That's what I mean by taking responsibility. Look, Doctor, a little bit of this sort of talk goes a long way with me. Can you . . ."

He squashed out his cigar and took another from the open tin immediately. Before he lit up, he risked a breath of air. It wasn't much of a risk in that room; the difference between smoking and not smoking was marginal. My eyes were beginning to water. The breath he took whistled and screeched like a train engine. He lit the cigar and inhaled quietly.

"I have never encountered a person more lacking in self-esteem than Paula Wilberforce. Nor one so adept at concealing the fact."

I shifted in my chair. "She followed me. She threatened me. She vandalized my car and stole my gun. She shot her father and shot up the house. I don't need to be told that she's disturbed. What I want to know is if she's ever said anything to you that will help me to locate her now."

"Possibly. Privileged information, but I might be prepared to divulge it on certain conditions."

"Try me."

"That you do everything in your power to see that she does not come to harm. That you do not allow a situation to develop in which she may be shot or driven to shoot herself. Anything like that."

"Sure. That's implicit in my agreement with her father."

"I want it to be *explicit* in your agreement with me."

"Why are you so . . . adamant, Doctor?"

"I told you. Her case is extremely rare, with many very interesting features. I had begun a study of it when she interrupted treatment. I believe that if I could resume treating her and gather more data, I would have the basis for a brilliant piece of research."

I stared at him. "You cold-blooded bastard."

He shrugged and blew smoke.

"Okay," I said. "I accept. What do you have to tell me?"

He held up his meaty hand. His murky eyes examined the back of his gold wedding ring. "You are thinking that my condition is easy to accept. How can it be enforced? You will do your best and no one can ask for more. I *am* asking for more."

It was my turn to shrug.

"I talked to Detective Sergeant Willis. A shrewd man in his way. I agreed to acting as consultant for the police in the matter of your psychological fitness to hold a private enquiry agent's license. Willis believes that such a report is in order, given your recent behavior."

"You set me up. You and Willis."

"You do see the point, don't you? Your best may not be good enough to enable you to hold your license. I understand professionalism, Mr. Hardy. Part of it involves looking ahead to the next project. Completing the one on hand, certainly, but learning from it and looking to the future. Unless you do better than your best, you won't have a future in your present career."

My eyes were watering badly, and my throat was becoming raw from breathing the smoke-laden air. I wanted out. "I understand," I rasped. "Tell me."

"Dogs," he said. "Somehow the key to her errant behavior lies in her attitude to dogs. Wherever she is now, whatever she is doing, dogs will be involved."

"Is that it? Dogs?"

He spread his hands, keeping the cigar imprisoned between two fingers. "I thought it might help."

"I thought you might tell me about a person—a friend, a lover, an enemy. Someone, some-where . . ."

"I'm sorry."

"Who is in most danger from her?"

"Other members of her family."

"Have you treated any of them?"

"I cannot possibly discuss such things with you."

"That means yes. Who?"

Another cigar died, and another was reborn. "My hands are tied."

"Dogs," I said. "Great. I'll have to make a

note of that." I made a mock movement of my hand toward my pocket and felt the photograph. I pulled it out, unfolded it, and laid it on the polished desk.

Holmes leaned forward to examine it.

"What would you say about this, Doc?"

"Paula's work?"

I nodded. "She did a painting too. I suspect she went at that with a hammer or a knife, maybe both."

Holmes blew smoke down at the photograph as he stared at it. I looked too. For an instant the shapes in the background threatened to make sense; then they returned to their enigmatic vagueness.

"This person is in grave danger. Who is he?"

I retrieved the picture and folded it up. "I couldn't possibly discuss that with you," I said.

16

I DROVE AWAY FROM WOOLLAHRA FEELING
that I'd accomplished something. By the time I
reached Glebe I couldn't think what the accom-
plishment might be. I had a vague feeling that
things were coming together, but nothing clearly
in my mind to justify the feeling. I've been in
this condition before, and my usual strategy involves a bottle, a ballpoint, and some paper. I
was still on antibiotics, and medical opinion
would be against the bottle. I remembered that I
hadn't taken the pills for the last twenty-four

hours, against all instructions. On the other hand, maybe the antibiotics accounted for my failure to see a pattern. It didn't seem like a good time to abandon a tested strategy.

Glen's car was parked outside the house. She wasn't due back until the next day, and the pessimist in me worried for an instant before the optimist in me was glad. I charged inside, scaring the cat from its sleep in the sun and putting a couple of the weak floorboards to the test. Glen was making coffee. She turned, and the smile on her face died.

I reached for her, but she held me back. "What's wrong?" I said. My first impulse was guilt, but I had nothing to be guilty about. Like Jimmy Carter, I'd sinned in my heart with Roberta, but that didn't count.

"When did you last look in a mirror, Cliff?"

"I dunno." I'd shaved under the shower in Bellevue Hill and combed my wet hair flat in the steamy bathroom. "Not lately."

"You look like death. Your color's bad. And you've got a tic."

"I do not have a tic." As I spoke, I lifted my hand to the nerve that was jumping in my cheek.

"What have you been doing?"

I slumped into a chair, feeling drained. "A lot, and nothing."

"I phoned last night, and when I got no answer, I was worried. I put a few things off and came back today."

I lifted my head to look at her. *Is this it?* I thought. *Is this where we have the fight that brings things to an end?* The possible reason was there. A man in my business can't have a little woman waiting at home for him or getting worried when the phone doesn't answer. Glen knew that, or at least I thought she did. We'd talked about it. Or had I just talked about it to myself? She was wearing civvies—skirt, blouse, heels—and she looked terrific. I wanted to touch her, to go up to bed with her and do our special things. I'd be a fool not to make concessions, not to make allowances for her concern. But . . .

Glen turned back to her coffee making. "I'm sorry," she said. "Didn't mean to be like that. It's only because you've been sick. Ordinarily you can do what you like. You know that."

Relief flooded through me. No crisis today. I got up and put my arms around her. "I know, love. Sorry to worry you. I spent the night with a couple of Wilberforces. Verity Lamberte's turned up. I took her into College Street today."

"I know. Good."

I kept my hold and kissed her clean, shining hair. I tried not to let her feel the irritation rising inside me. I didn't want my movements monitored like that. She turned around, and we kissed.

"D'you want coffee?"

"Later. I want something else first."

"You don't look as if you're up to it. Really, Cliff, you don't look well."

"I'm well," I said. "Try me."

We went upstairs and made love very gently, taking our time, avoiding my tender spots and trying to give each other maximum pleasure. We were both aware that a bad moment had passed. That made a good moment better.

Glen was right about my appearance and physical condition. The damaged parts of my back were inflamed, bordering on infection. In some places the skin was raw and weeping. Glen changed the dressings, which I had neglected, and applied ointment. I took catch-up doses of the antibiotics and aspirin for my slight fever. I drank some light beer and wine and tried to show how tough I was by insisting on watching the news on the portable TV and making caustic comments about Greiner. I fell asleep before they got to the sports and weather and slept the clock around, waking up at 6:00 A.M. to a wet dawn and crashing down again for another three hours.

When I got downstairs, I found that Glen had left. I prowled around, fearing a note, half wishing she'd left one. She hadn't. My tough-as-nails cop. I moped through the morning, reading old newspapers and putting off the time when I'd have to sit down with the ballpoint and paper. Frank Parker rang in solicitous mood, and I broke it by telling him about the deal struck between Willis and Dr. Holmes.

"Why not, Cliff? Willis has to get a handle on you somehow. People blown up in mountain shacks. Loaded pistols floating about. I admire his sense of endeavor."

"Shit, Frank. I'm up to my balls in questions with no answers. And my livelihood is on the line."

"That's the way it should be. This is a deregulated society, haven't you heard? The public sector has to justify every cent spent. That's tough, believe me. The private sector has to compete sixty seconds a minute, sixty minutes an hour, twenty-four hours a day, seven days a—"

"Bullshit."

"Yeah, I know. Is there any way I can help, Cliff?"

"I thought you'd never ask. Complete police records on Paula Wilberforce, Verity Lamberte, Patrick Lamberte, Sir Phillip Wilberforce, Nadia Crosbie, Robert Crosbie, and Rudi, the dog. Also, all changes of address and movements for the past twenty years."

The pen scratch noise I could hear on the line stopped. "I'm glad you're joking, Cliff. That's impossible."

"I know. But you asked."

"I'll get you what I can. You want me to have a word with Willis?"

"No. How's Hilde?"

"A sweet point in a sour world. Glen?"

"The same. Thanks, Frank. Hope to hear from you."

The sky cleared suddenly, the way it will in July, and I went for a walk. Glebe was getting progressively more like Woollahra, but there were still significant differences—like beer cans in the gutters and the TAB doing a roaring trade in the middle of the day. A council worker was sweeping in Boyce Street. He kept moving, but he seemed to be more concerned to make a certain number of broom strokes per yard than with the effect. He covered the territory, but a good part of the rubbish remained behind.

I leaned on the fence at the end of Boyce Street and looked out over the Harold Park paceway. A few trotters circled the track quietly. Ground staff were moving around the gardens, betting areas, and stands, watering and cleaning, making it a pleasant place for people to lose money at in a few hours. I'd lost a good bit there myself over the years. I considered dropping in at the busy TAB and consulting the form. I didn't. I could pretend that the Wilberforce-Lamberte matter was just another case, deserving of my best efforts but nothing more. Dr. Holmes had upped the ante, but he really needn't have bothered. The ante was high enough for me already. I had to *know*.

I'd spent a couple of hours with the pen and paper by the time Glen got home. I'd got nowhere. She touched my head as she walked past and didn't disturb me. It felt strange. So much consideration and my not doing anything to deserve it. I struggled with frustration and building ill temper.

"I'm going out," Glen said. "Police thing. I might be late."

"Okay."

We were both on edge, wanting to leave it there—professional on both sides, no worries. I couldn't. She came down the stairs wearing a blue dress that I liked her in and carrying a black velvet jacket over her shoulder.

"You look lovely," I said. "Will there be dancing?"

She laughed. "No."

"Good. Will the nineteen-year-olds with the pectorals and laterals and transversal joints be there?"

"Uh-uh. It's for pooh-bahs. Community policing policy—pollies, the odd mayor, you know."

I got up, and we drew close for some of the touching and nuzzling that should remind us that we're only animals. We were both still wary, though.

"Well, I'll be off." She couldn't find an easy exit line, and she looked at the papers and bits and pieces I'd been playing with. She pointed. "What's that?"

I picked up the photograph and handed it to her. "It's Patrick Lamberte photographed by

Paula Wilberforce. The only questions are where, when, and why."

"It's in the country somewhere. That's a tree and that's a sort of gully."

I followed her finger as it traced shapes on the surface, shapes I hadn't even seen before.

"I think you're right. In the country. Well, that rules out Darlo."

"Don't be a prick, Cliff. I can't help it if you're short of ideas."

Glen has the sort of eyes that can see ships over the horizon. She'd had no trouble spotting the dead ends indicated by my doodlings. She held the photograph up to the light and looked hard at it.

"Summer, to judge from the shadows."

"What shadows?"

"There. Dark ones."

"Oh, yeah. I don't suppose you've got any idea what those shapes in the background are?"

"Dogs," Glen said.

I went back to my notes and doodles. I wondered what was taught at the Petersham College of TAFE about this sort of situation. What was the reading list for Running out of Ideas I and

Dead Ends IIA? The cat decided it was time to leave its place by the radiator and walk across my papers.

"Scratch about a bit," I told it. "Maybe you can get this stuff into an arrangement that makes sense."

The cat sat down on top of the mysterious photograph and brushed my pen off the table with its tail.

"Big help," I said.

Frank Parker rang soon after. "I did a bit of looking around for you," he said. "Nothing much came up. One thing, there was Nadia Crosbie who drowned in Queensland a few years back. Is that yours?"

"Yes."

"Seems there was something fishy about that, no pun intended. The local police weren't entirely satisfied about the circumstances: suspicious person seen in the vicinity, weather conditions, state of the body—that sort of thing. All circumstantial. Nothing came of it. The police up there had other things to worry about at the time. The coroner returned death by misadventure, but I just thought you might like to know."

I thanked him, recovered my pen, and scribbled the date of Nadia Crosbie's death—2 June

1989—on a piece of paper not covered by cat. The cat got offended and jumped off the table. I looked at the notes again. It was risky being a Wilberforce-Lamberte-Crosbie. It was risky being a Hardy. Safer to be a cat.

I got a glass of wine and had one more shot at it, hoping for the lightbulb to glow. It didn't. Among the scribble a name written in block capitals stood out. "CLIVE STEPHENSON." Who the hell was he? Then I remembered that he was Patrick Lamberte's solicitor. His address was in the same building as Cy Sackville, my long-suffering lawyer. Maybe Cy could help me there. That was probably what was taught at TAFE: When in doubt, ring your lawyer.

17

THE WORDS OF A SONG WERE RUNNING through my head as I waited to be ushered into the presence of Clive Stephenson with a *ph:* "In ten years' time we'll have one million lawyers . . . how much can a poor nation stand?" Cy Sackville had arranged for me to see Stephenson at very short notice.

"After a bit of persuasion Clive said he'd find a window in his diary," Cy had told me.

"What?"

"That's the way he talks. Went to law school

in Chicago. When he looks out at the harbor, I think he pretends it's the Great Lakes."

"How should I handle him?"

"Flatter him. If that doesn't work, insult him. Clive's not a subtle guy, but he has got a sense of humor. He owes me a favor or two. He'll play along with you as far as he can."

"What's his field?"

"Company law, what else?"

"Is he interested in due process of law, justice for all, getting to the truth, or money?"

"Ha," Cy had said.

Stephenson was older-looking than I had expected, although maybe he was just practicing looking like a judge. He wore a dark suit, striped tie, and his hair was a distinguished shade of gray at the sides. His office was supertraditional with an American flavor. Everything Clarence Darrow would have had was there, except perhaps for the cuspidor. He sat me down opposite his desk. I refused coffee.

"How can I help you, Mr. Hardy?" He had a deep voice with an educated Australian accent plus a touch of the Midwest. Pity he wasn't a barrister.

"You represent the late Patrick Lamberte?"

He nodded. Saving the voice for when it was most needed.

"Mrs. Lamberte hired me to inquire into certain aspects of her husband's dealings. I was present when the house at Mount Victoria burned down."

"Tragic business. What exactly were you looking into?"

"I can't tell you precisely, but Mrs. Lamberte was afraid that her husband intended to harm her. Does that surprise you?"

He shook his head. For a minute I thought he was conserving the voice box again, but I was wrong. "It doesn't surprise me one bit," he said. "I've never seen a couple so divided, so fundamentally hostile to each other." He pronounced it "hostel."

"You think he was capable of killing her?"

"In certain moods, yes. But Lamberte was a pretty controlled character, really. He was in a lot of financial and personal trouble and wouldn't have wanted any more."

"How much financial trouble?"

He opened his hands. "Plenty. But he had a chance of getting out of it."

"If his wife didn't take him for fifty percent?"

"It wouldn't have helped."

"The Family Court proceedings would have been tricky?"

"Bloody. Where's this leading? If you're working for Mrs. Lamberte, you'll find out all about her husband's affairs in due course. She gets the estate, what there is of it. I'm liaising with Brian Garfield on that."

"I'm not exactly working for Mrs. Lamberte just now."

He leaned back in his chair and touched the gray streaks in a way that made me suspect that they were cosmetic. "I don't follow."

"I'm actually working for Sir Phillip Wilberforce, trying to locate his daughter. There's a connection between her and Lamberte." I hated myself for the "Sir Phillip," but I forgave myself.

There is no category of human being more monarchist and pro-aristocracy than a Republican American, which is what Stephenson was aping. He was impressed. "What kind of connection? The obvious?"

"I know Lamberte was sexually active," I said. "But Paula Wilberforce apparently wasn't. I suspect it wasn't about sex, or not altogether. I'm fishing, I admit. Did he ever mention her to you? Does her name appear on any documents you've seen?"

He shook his head. "No, to both questions. I'd remember the name."

"I know very little about him. Were you friends, or what?"

"He designed my house. That's how we met."

"Good house?"

"For now. It's at Bowral. Patrick owned some country property himself, and he'd put up a few nice houses on acres, if you know what I mean."

"Bowral," I said.

He glanced at his Rolex. "I'm sorry. I'm afraid I'm going to have to—"

"You said Bowral. Did Lamberte own land at Bowral? I thought he'd had to sell everything off?"

His carefully controlled face became cagey. "Is that what Mrs. Lamberte told you?"

I nodded.

"That's right, he did. But when he was riding high and the banks were ladling out the money, he bought and speculated like Donald Trump. He had property all over the place. I'm not sure of the exact state of his holdings as of now."

I could hear the bells ringing and feel the synapses being bridged. "Now doesn't matter," I said. "If you could dig out a list of Lamberte's property holdings at his peak, it could help tremendously."

Stephenson stroked his closely shaven chin. "I don't know."

"How can it hurt? The guy's dead."

Stephenson's grin was wolfish. The sense of humor Cy had alleged to exist flashed into sight. "And his account's way overdue. I've got people to see, Mr. Hardy, but I'm sure I can oblige you. Why don't you step outside and ask for Robin?" He gave me his wise-as-Clarence-Darrow smile and picked up the phone.

"Robin, would you get the Lamberte file up on screen for Mr. Hardy, please? Specifically assets. Okay? Many thanks."

Back in the busy outer office, I deduced that Robin was the woman looking at a VDT while keeping one eye on Stephenson's door. She raised a hand and beckoned me over. I approached warily. I have mixed feelings about computers: I like them when they save me time and effort; I hate them when they get between me and something I want, like my money on a Saturday afternoon.

Robin was about twenty-two and probably

couldn't remember the precomputer age. She surrendered her chair to me and pointed at the screen. "There you go. Assets."

She started to move away, but I took hold of her arm and held her. "I don't know how to work this thing."

"It's simple." She picked up a plastic object the size of a cigarette pack. "You can use a mouse or the keyboard."

"I haven't got any cheese and I don't play the piano."

She blinked, then smiled hesitantly. "A joke, right?"

"Right. But I still don't know how to run a computer."

"Sit down. Here's the cursor, see? You move it up and down with these arrow keys and the information scrolls."

"Cute," I said.

"Call me if you have a problem."

She went across the room and whispered in the ear of a young man sitting at a desk. He glanced across at me, and they both laughed. I'd like to see them drive an '81 Falcon manual.

My assets would have taken up about three lines; Patrick Lamberte's filled the screen several times over. I scrolled carefully through it. His basic company, Lamberte Holdings, had subsidiaries like Pat Co. and Verity Inc. There was a Shane Trust and a Michelle Pty Ltd. It was hard to tell how solid the assets were without knowing the meaning of the code numbers that accompanied them. If 0026 meant "wholly owned and in the black," Patrick was in good shape; if it meant "money owing," he was down the tubes.

On the third screenful I found it: Fitzroy House Kennels, owned by the Shane Trust. I looked up and caught Robin watching me. She raised an eyebrow, I nodded, and she hurried over. Very economical this computer business. I pointed to the item on the screen. "How do I get more information?"

Automatically her hand snaked out and her long-nailed fingers began tapping the keys. The print on the screen changed from white on blue to black on white. Fitzroy House Kennels was located at Lot 5, Wombeyan Road, between Bowral and Mittagong. That was the only part of the text that made sense to me; the rest was columns of figures and more code numbers.

I made a note of the address and looked helplessly at Robin. "What does it mean?"

She did some more key tapping. "Doesn't make any money. Never did. Bought in 1986 for three hundred thousand, top of the boom that'd be. Mortgaged . . . let's see, probably above its current value. Westpac and others. If you're interested in buying it, you can probably pick it up for a song."

"Are you a lawyer or an economist, Robin?"

"Both."

"Kennels," I said. "Dog minding?"

"Supposedly. Dog and cat minding. But it hasn't operated for a couple of years, and the rates haven't been paid, see?" She touched a key, and the screen filled with copies of correspondence.

"Does it have a manager, a tenant, or whatever?"

Another key stroke, another display. "Walked out early last year. Owing rent."

"So there's no one there now?"

"I guess. Do you want a survey map?"

"Why not?"

A stretch appeared on screen. Robin hit some keys, and a printer across the room began chattering. She went over to it and tore off a sheet. She went to her own desk, folded the map, and put it in an envelope. I got up and began to tell her that the envelope wasn't necessary. She smiled and asked me for my name and address. I gave them, and her fingers flew across the keyboard of her computer.

"What's that for?"

"We'll bill you," she said.

I stood in Martin Place, shortly before lunchtime. A few brave souls were settling down on the seats with their lunches, turning their backs to the cold wind. I walked down Pitt Street and went into the first pub I came to. I bought a scotch and took it across to a table as far from the blaring TV set as I could get. I opened the long white envelope and looked at the annotated survey map. The property known as Fitzroy House consisted of a sandstone cottage built in the northern quadrant of a 4.5 hectare allotment. Improvements comprised a large garage, swimming pool, tennis court, and "buildings erected for the purpose of caring for domestic pets." The block had a creek running through it, and it fronted onto Wombeyan Road for 339 feet.

I tried to work out how many acres there were in 4.5 hectares. A lot. The cottage was built in 1883; there were probably quite a few rooms in it. A good out-of-the-way place to hide. Good for dogs, too.

18

IT WAS RAINING BY THE TIME I GOT BACK TO
Glebe, but I had everything I needed to cope
with that. I changed out of the sort of clothes you
wear to visit a lawyer into the sort you wear to go
looking for a madwoman in the country: boots,
thick socks, jeans, and a sweater. The good-qual-
ity parka I'd got from Terry Reeves had been
reduced to a burned ruin, so I took mine, older,
less padded, hoodless. I still had the leather
jacket, except that it had lain as a soggy mess in
the back of the Cruiser for a couple of days. I

collected a few more items, like my antibiotic capsules, and then I had to ask myself the question: Did I compound my lawbreaking by taking the unregistered Colt with me? The thought of Paula Wilberforce's blue eyes gave me the answer.

I left a note for Glen, including the car phone number, telling her that I could be away overnight. Through the kitchen window I could see that the rain was driving down hard and it was getting dark in the midafternoon. It didn't matter. I'd have gone if it had been snowing.

On the road I was glad of the big vehicle's tire traction, powerfully sweeping wipers, and sure handling. The rain was coming down in sheets from a leaden sky, and I tried to remember the last weather forecast I had heard or read. Nothing had stuck. I turned on the radio and got one: rain, rain, and more rain; flood warnings on the south coast, cold nights. Somewhere out near Campbelltown the cars with weak wipers and lights were pulling over to the side of the road. If I'd been driving the Falcon, I'd have been with them. Better a wet distributor and a long wait than a pileup in the mist. The rain didn't slacken, but the traffic adjusted to it. The trucks labored along in the left lane, the speedsters

curbed themselves, and we 4WD men were the
kings of the road.

Although the freeway was built years ago, I still
think of it as new because I drove the old road
many, many more times. It bypasses all the
towns, but I still measure the distance and know
where I am in terms of them. It was somewhere
past Picton that the blue and red flashing lights
began appearing and the wail of sirens lifted
above the noise of tires and wipers. Every vehicle on the road slowed down to allow the ambu-
lances and police cars through, and we all drove
circumspectly past the place where four cars had
collided. They were slewed around on the road
—headlights pointing crazily and rear bumpers
and radiators crumpled and leaking plastic and
metal.

People huddled by the side of the road, their
faces white in the headlights; cops, with water
sloshing off their yellow slickers, were directing
the traffic; and paramedics, shielded by umbrel-
las held over them, dealt with the still shapes
stretched out on the wet tarmac.

I stopped at one of the big highway service
centers that have replaced petrol stations and

truckies' cafés. It was all neon and glass and aluminum—easy-to-clean surfaces that were still new and bright but would one day become as dull as the old café lamina. The place was doing good business. I suspected that a lot of the customers were drivers who were hoping for the rain to stop. Others, shaken up by the accident scene, needed to get off the road for the sake of their nerves. I wasn't sure which category I was in. I ordered coffee and a hamburger from a uniformed girl behind the counter. No waiting. The stuff was hot and ready to go. I took the polystyrene box into a corner and sat with my back to the road. Maybe I was in category two.

As I sat there, I examined my certainty that Paula Wilberforce was hiding at Fitzroy House. I decided that there was no basis for it in fact, just an enormously high probability. It felt right. On the other matter—whether she'd killed Patrick Lamberte and Karen Livermore—I felt no certainty at all. It seemed unlikely, but so did the deaths themselves. Halfway through the hamburger I realized I was hungry. I hadn't had lunch. I was supposed to take the antibiotics before meals, but what if you didn't have meals? I took a couple of capsules anyway and washed them down with a second cup of coffee.

I used the toilet and examined myself in the mirror. Pale from lack of sun, a bit hollow-eyed, and sunken-cheeked. No oil painting. No photograph. Back in the Land Cruiser with the rain still coming down, I phoned Glen, using the gizmo. No answer. I phoned the Wilberforce house in Randwick and got Mrs. Darcy. I asked her how her patient was doing.

"Not well, Mr. Hardy. The doctor's been and seems very concerned about him."

"What's the problem?"

"Irregular breathing and pulse. He seems to be weakening."

"Is he conscious?"

"Oh, yes. He's reading, and he demands whiskey from time to time. The doctor says he might as well have it."

That *was* a bad sign. I asked her if he'd mentioned me or Paula. "There was something he was trying to remember."

"He mentioned you only to ask if you had been in touch. I don't suppose you have any good news for him? I believe it would help."

I told her I didn't, not yet, but that I might have soon. I gave her the mobile phone number and asked her to give old Phil my best wishes. Glen didn't answer either at Glebe or Petersham.

Well, why the hell should she? We were independent adults, weren't we? Pursuing our own fates. I filled up with unleaded and got back out on the road. It was seven o'clock, and the traffic was thinner. The rain slanting down through the beam of the headlights was steady and being moved around by a slight wind. The heater and defroster were doing their jobs. I was doing mine, but whether coming up with good news was part of it or not I didn't know.

As the road climbed, the rain began to clear. A few miles out of Mittagong it was a drizzle; by the same distance on the other side of the town it had stopped. At Mittagong I turned off the freeway. The sky was clear, and the moon was bright and almost full. Even the stars seemed to be giving out some helpful light, but that might have been my imagination; it was just so good to see the rain stop. I found Wombeyan Road at the midpoint of the old route to Bowral and turned off a reasonably wide, reasonably well-lit bitumen strip onto a narrow, rutted track from which the tarmac was fast falling away. After a mile or two it gave up trying and became a dirt road.

Tall gums growing along both sides of the road

cut down the light, and I had trouble locating the lot numbers. Why should the owners bother? Everyone who lived along Wombeyan Road knew who was where; others could please themselves. There was no traffic, and I had the feeling that I'd entered an alien landscape and was all alone. City boy feeling. The glimpses I had through the trees of the properties behind them weren't encouraging. A few dim lights in the far distance; dark shapes, probably cows, on gentle, moonlit slopes—good country for hiding, bad country for searching.

The 4WD's strong headlights picked up the sign hanging lopsidedly from a tree branch. One of the chains supporting it had snapped, and the board had dropped almost to the ground on that side. Years, weather, and the Australia-wide rural habit of using signs as rifle targets had ravaged it, but something of its original charm was still visible: A dog and a cat stood nose to muzzle against a background of rolling hills. FITZROY HOUSE KENNELS was written above them in a ye-olde-English script. The name of the proprietor and the telephone number had been obliterated by bullet holes.

The property had once boasted a white post and rail fence. This was now a rotted ruin, rapidly fading to a neutral gray and sagging back toward the earth. The gateposts leaned drunkenly inward, leaving only a narrow entry. Wide enough for the Land Cruiser, but only just. I steered it through and ran down the eroded track for a few yards before pulling off into the shelter of the scrub beside it. I turned off the engine and the lights and stared out through the windshield into the silent darkness. One fact about the place I had entered had registered strongly: Although the track sprouted high weeds and was overgrown from both sides, other vehicles had passed down it recently.

I stepped down into a cold that I hadn't really expected. The cessation of the rain had lulled me into a feeling that the outside world was benign. Instead, it was colder than in the mountains. A steady, knife-edged wind blew from the south. It cut through three layers of clothing and chilled my feet immediately. I forced myself to open the back of the Cruiser and search for the things I needed: torch, matches, groundsheet, gloves. My fingers were stiff and clumsy, and I fumbled in the dark, touching icy metal and cursing softly when the object proved not to be what I wanted.

I heard it before I saw or felt it: The dog must

have growled as it launched itself into a tremendous spring. I reacted instinctively, throwing myself to one side and holding on to whatever my hand touched in hopes that it was a weapon. The velocity of the dog's leap and the vigor of its attack on the padded thickness of my parka almost pulled me down. It wrenched its jaws free of the material and sprang again, directly at my face. I screamed and threw up my hands. I was holding the soggy, mildewed leather jacket and the dog's teeth fastened on it. It snarled and let go as it realized that old, wet leather wasn't fresh meat. I stepped back, still holding the jacket which was now minus a sleeve. I tried to wrap it around my arm in the approved fashion, but the dog was on me again, snapping and attacking low.

I kicked it and connected solidly, only enraging the animal. It howled and threw itself at me. I knew that if it got me down, I'd be finished; probably howling myself, I flailed at it with the jacket. I felt the weight of the Colt in my pocket and struggled to get it out while the dog backed off with another chunk of leather and lining in its jaws. I got the gun free, and when the dog jumped again, I hit it as hard as I could, bringing the gun butt down on its head. The blow glanced off bone and gouged into an eye socket. The dog seemed to turn in midair and attack again without having touched ground. I pounded the gun against the side of its head, mashing an ear. It snarled and grabbed my ankle. I beat down at it, feeling bone and flesh turn soft and pulpy until its grip relaxed.

I leaned back against the Land Cruiser, breathing hard. My breath made clouds of steam in the icy air, but I was sweating. Perspiration trickled down my body. My hair was prickling all over my scalp and I could feel the adrenaline pumping through me like an electric current. The dog twitched and thrashed, then lay still. It was a big yellow dog. I like dogs, but the feeling has to be mutual. Years ago I had to shoot one that was attacking me. This was worse, and there was a single thought in my head: *Are there any more of them?* I wasn't sure I could go through it again.

The phone bleeped. I staggered around to the cabin, jerked open the door, and picked up the instrument in my left hand. My right was locked around the Colt as if it would never let go.

"Yes."

"Cliff, it's Glen. Are you all right?"

"I've just beaten an attack dog to death."

"My God, where are you? I'll get some people to you. Cliff, where are you?"

"I'm okay," I said.

"You're not. You sound terrible. Cliff . . ."

She was right. I wasn't okay. My pulse was racing, and the sweat was freezing on my body. I was trembling as I stood there, and I didn't know whether it was from the cold or fear or relief. All I knew was that I was going on with what I'd started.

"I'm okay," I said again. "Don't worry." I slammed the phone back into its housing.

No more yellow, snarling shapes came hurtling from the darkness. The wind blew steadily; the light scrub seemed to bend aside to let it through. I wondered if it snowed out here. If so, this could be the night. My pulse rate and breathing returned to normal. I stepped over the carcass of the dog and returned to the job of collecting things from the back of the Cruiser. To do so, I had to release my grip on the Colt. I shoved it back in the pocket of the torn parka and found the gloves and a knitted cap. With their protection, things didn't seem so bad. I contemplated taking the phone with me, but if there was a way of muting its ring I didn't know about it, and I didn't fancy having it bleeping away unexpectedly.

Torch in hand, I moved along the track in the direction of the house. I knew it would be a fairly long tramp, but I couldn't risk taking the vehicle any closer. I'd studied the survey map, but things are very different on the ground and in the dark. I didn't know for certain where the kennels were located; I wasn't even sure where the creek was. If Paula Wilberforce was here, she certainly had the advantage of knowing the territory. For my part, I had military training, a lot of experience in dangerous situations, and a very high regard for my personal safety when I stopped to think about it. I also had a bigger gun and, very likely, more bullets.

The house loomed up suddenly like a mountain. "Cottage" had given me the wrong impression. It was a three-story job with a high-pitched roof and several chimneys. The moonlight gave it a certain grandeur, but even so, I could see that it was almost a ruin. Windows were boarded up, creeper had invaded the masonry and guttering on one side, and at least one section of the veranda, which appeared to run right around the building, had collapsed. The front porch was heaped high with wooden pallets and bales of barbed wire. From where I stood I couldn't see how to get into the house or even if entry was possible. I moved closer and risked a quick flash of the torch. The veranda threatened to collapse completely any second, and the wall I was looking at had a crack from top to bottom wide enough to put your fist in.

I circled the building, keeping twenty yards away, stepping through overgrown garden beds and across cracked cement paths. A garden hose, attached to a tap, but otherwise covered in weeds, almost tripped me up. I swore as I stumbled, and then I went to ground deliberately. Something or someone, off to my left, was moving toward the house. I squinted through the weeds. My first feeling was of relief: The figure was human. I lifted myself a little to get a better look. A tall person wearing a long coat with a hood pulled up stopped ten yards short of the house and gave a long, low whistle.

"Rudi. Rudi."

I recognized the voice and got to my feet. As I did, she turned in my direction. The hood fell away, and the moonlight caught on her blond hair, turning it silvery. Suddenly she was the younger female image of her father.

"Paula." I moved quickly toward her, watching carefully: If her hand moved toward her coat pocket . . .

She stood stock-still. "Who's that?"

I pulled off the cap. "Don't be scared. It's Hardy."

I was only a few yards away now. She glared at me and took her hands out of the folds of the long scarf she wore around her neck. "Where's Rudi?"

"What?"

"Where's my dog?"

I couldn't say, "Out on the track with his brains beaten in." I didn't say anything. She got closer, and those blue eyes transfixed me. I dropped the torch to the ground, unzipped the parka for easier access to the Colt.

"You're covered in blood. You've killed him, you bastard!"

She threw herself forward, clawing for my eyes with fingers bent like grappling hooks. I stepped back to give myself space to grab her wrists. I got one, missed the other, and her fingernails raked my face from cheekbone to jaw. She was a fury with the strength of a man. I wrestled with her there in the weeds, struggling to avoid her flailing, slashing right hand, trying to imprison it while she wrenched and jerked, trying to get the other hand free. She swore and spit and kicked at me; she had long legs and wore heavy shoes. She caught me solidly on the ankle the dog had bitten, and I yelled. I clubbed her with a roundhouse right that took her behind the ear and made her gasp. Only gasp. I didn't want to hit her with a real punch, but it was beginning to look as if I'd have to. She got the left hand free, and I knew it would be coming for my eyes in a split second. I slapped her right cheek hard and stepped aside. She rushed forward, and I tripped her. She fell hard, facedown into the grass, and I straddled her, pinning her wrists together behind her back.

I was panting again, belching out steam and feeling pressure build in every part of my body. I licked my lips and tasted blood. The wound on my face was stinging in the icy air, and I could feel the blood dripping from my face to join the dog's blood on the parka. She bucked and heaved like Benny Elias after a tackle. She almost threw me off, but I scrabbled for better balance and a better grip with my boots on either side of her wildly thrashing body.

"Murderer," she moaned. "Fuck you."

I let her feel some more of my weight.

"Give it up, Paula. Give it up."

"I'll kill you." Her voice was muffled by grass and dirt. "I'll rip your throat out."

"You won't," I said. "I'll put some pressure on your neck and you'll pass out. Then I'll unwind your scarf and tie you up. Is that what you want?"

I felt the cold metal against the nape of my neck and simultaneously heard the man's voice. "It's not what *she* wants that matters, Hardy. It's what *I* want."

19

"OH, JESUS," PAULA GASPED. "ROBERT! What the hell are you doing here? Get him off me, will you? I'm freezing to death."

"Maybe that'd be the best thing all round," Robert Crosbie said. "If you freeze to death underneath Hardy, who's found dead with a bullet in the back of his neck."

"Don't be an idiot. Tell him to get off me."

I could smell him close behind me, but I couldn't tell exactly where he was. He'd moved the gun a fraction so that I wasn't sure where it was either.

"Shut up, bitch!" His voice was nasally harsh. "I knew he'd come, and anyone with half a brain'd know a fucking dog wouldn't stop him. If it was anything like the first Rudi, the world's a better place for its being dead."

Fury beneath me: squealing, wriggling, heaving.

"I can't hold her, Crosbie," I said.

He laughed. "You'll hold her, and you'll do exactly as you said. Get her scarf and tie her up."

"Robert!"

She protested, but it was me he swiped with the gun. I felt the muzzle cut my scalp, and I wanted to get up and take him on, but I didn't. Tying her up seemed like a good idea. I yanked the scarf free and made a good job of it, lashing her wrists together and making the knots hard and tight. I risked a glance behind me as I did it, but Robert was in control. He'd backed off a yard, and his right hand was nicely extended and balanced.

"Okay," I said. "She's secure."

"Right. Now take off your parka."

"What?"

"Don't talk, just do it. I learned this in the

reserves. Use the environment to make your enemy as uncomfortable as possible. I'd call this environment cold, wouldn't you? Strip it off! Left arm first."

I did it slowly, trying to give myself time to resolve a dilemma. If he felt the weight of the parka, he'd know there was a gun in it. I'd only seen his gun out of the corner of my eye, but it might have been a .38, which meant it might be mine. And that was a one-shot gun at best. Unwise to give him another eight rounds. I slipped out of the parka and threw it away. It landed noiselessly in the grass.

"Now get off her."

I eased myself up and turned slowly to face him. He was wearing a balaclava, padded jacket, and thick pants tucked into fur-lined boots. The pistol was scarcely visible in his gloved hand. Maybe a .38, and maybe mine, but only maybe.

He moved very quickly. Before I had time to think about evasion or attack, he'd slipped behind Paula and hauled her to her feet. The pistol was jammed into her ear.

"She's what you came to find, isn't she? What you'll get paid for?"

"Yes."

"Bastard!" Paula hissed, but at which one of us it was impossible to tell.

"Well then, do as I say or all you'll give that old bastard is another funeral to go to. Did you kill the dog, Hardy?"

I was acutely aware of the woman standing like a statue in Crosbie's grip. Another dilemma. If I admitted to killing the dog, she'd almost certainly react and he'd kill her.

"What dog?" I said.

Crosbie chuckled. "She said you were covered with dog's blood."

I was shivering violently. The wind was still blowing hard, and without the parka I felt as if it were freezing my marrow. I slapped my arms against my sides. "This is crazy," I said. "Let me get my coat."

Crosbie's gun hand didn't move an inch, which showed me that he knew what he was doing.

"No," he said. "I think we'll go to the kennels. Paula likes dogs so much, let's see how she likes being in a kennel."

He laughed and nudged Paula into movement. We walked slowly along a cement path away from the house, away from my Colt, toward madness. Paula went without a struggle, surprising me. The thought came to me that it was all an act, something being staged by the two of them to control me. It was a tempting thought, but I had to reject it. Crosbie's voice and the grip he held Paula in were for real. Accepting that, I began to worry even more. My .38 has a very light action; if Crosbie stumbled or sneezed, Paula could be history. I thought of telling him so, but the calm assurance of his movements was one of the things that prevented me. Another was the certainty that fear would show in my voice. I was very scared.

And cold. The wind seemed to be separating my ribs and blowing through the gaps. I wrapped my arms around my chest and kept moving. The path ended at a long, low building, something like a stable. It was made of brick and divided into compartments, each with a heavy grille gate about three feet high. Above the gates, reaching to the roof, the front of each compartment was made of timber. There looked to be a dozen or so of these stalls; the gates of the first three stood open.

Crosbie stopped at the first gate. "Bend over, Hardy, and get in there."

"No," Paula said. "That's Rudi's house."

"Do it, Hardy. Or I swear I'll kill her on the spot."

It was now or never. I had to do something. "You won't kill her."

"I've killed three people already. What difference will one more make? Or two for that matter."

I bent and turned slightly, ready to jump at him, but he was still too far away and too poised. "I'll freeze to death in there."

Again the laugh, sounding slightly crazy now. "Old Rudi must've had a blanket. Might be a few fleas in it, but you'll be okay. Move!"

I bent double and went through the gate. He kicked it closed, and I heard a lock click solidly into place. There was a scuffling noise and the sound of a slap. Then his boot hit the next gate and the lock engaged. I crouched by the gate, looking out at the bricked yard in front of the kennels. Crosbie had put the gun away somewhere and was straightening his clothes. He looked extremely pleased with himself. I suppose he had a right to be.

"How did you get here, Hardy?"

"I flew."

He disappeared from my sight. I heard a sound I couldn't interpret, and then a stream of icy water hit me in the chest. I banged my head on the low roof as I retreated to the back of the kennel and Crosbie played the hose through the grille, searching for me. I tripped over something on the concrete floor and fell. My head hit the brick wall.

"Now you *are* in trouble. I think I've wet your blanket."

"Robert, Robert, don't leave me here, please. I'll do anything you say." Paula's voice trembled and broke.

Crosbie chuckled. "You're a lousy actress, Paula. You always were. You never fooled anyone except that fucking father of yours."

Paula moaned. "If only I had Rudi. I'd like to watch him eat your eyes."

"Your cellmate killed him, remember? I think I'd better go and collect your vehicle, Hardy. You're a predictable sort of bloke. I think I'll be able to find it."

"I'll kill you, Robert. I swear I'll kill you."

"You had your try at killing, Paula. You fucked it up the way you fuck up everything. Just wait around awhile, I might let you kill Mr. Hardy here."

He threw the hose down and stamped off the way we'd come. My shirt and pants were wet, and the cold was numbing me. I flapped my arms and skinned the knuckles of my left hand on the bricks. My head hurt, my back hurt, and my pride was groveling in the dirt somewhere. Bent over, I explored the kennel. It was solid brick; the timber planks in the front were morticed into the brick pillars. The iron roof had been nailed down by an expert; there was no give in it at all. In the back wall there was a section of thick glass bricks to admit light. They were as solidly mortared as the rest of the structure. I picked up the sodden blanket and wrapped it around my shoulder. It smelled of dog, but it afforded some warmth.

"Paula."

No answer.

"Paula, talk to me. He's crazy. You know that. Tell me just one thing. Is that my gun he's got?"

"What does it matter, arsehole?"

"It matters. If it's my gun, it's probably only got one bullet in it. See the point?"

Even through her anger she couldn't fail to understand that.

"It could be your gun. I left it in my car. Robert might have found it. It could be the gun I tried to kill my father with."

"We won't go into that now." I rattled the gate

to my cage. "Christ, these things are solid. Why did they have to build them so strong?"

"You think any old shitty place'll do for animals, don't you? You fucker."

"Paula, shut up! We have to think of something. You heard him, he's killed three people. When did he turn up here anyway? I take it you've been here since you—"

"Since I shot Dad. Yes. I don't know when he got here. The first I knew was when he put that fucking gun to your dumb head. This is a big place; there's a couple of other buildings to shelter in. What three people did he kill? Who's dead?"

The flat, uninvolved way she spoke worried me. It was as if she'd lost interest in the human race. It was hard to know how to answer. Instinct told me to hedge.

"What was your connection with Patrick Lamberte? I saw a photo you took of him. You'd . . . disfigured it."

"I hate him! Oh, he was charming for a while. We came out here and looked over the place. And then do you know what he did? He threw the man who was caring for the animals here out, and he let the dogs die. Ten of them. A couple got loose and went wild, after being starved till they went mad. I've loathed him ever since then."

"You took a picture of him here and did a painting."

"That was when he was being nice. When he first bought this place. I thought he was going to preserve it, make it happy again and take care of the dogs—"

She broke off and sobbed. I shivered in my wet blanket. The hose, still running water, was lying on the bricks close to the gate. I wondered if I could stick my arm through and get it. What was the point?

"Lamberte's dead," I said. "He died in a fire up at Mount Victoria. Karen Livermore died with him. Remember Karen?"

"You're pronouncing it wrongly," she said dully. "It's Kah-ren. Sure I remember her. Stupid to the bone, like her mother. Did Robert kill them? Good. Who else, Hardy? This is good. Who else? I'll bet it wasn't Verity. Not Verity."

"Why d'you say that?" I was straining my ears for the sound of a motor, a hard thing to do when your teeth are chattering violently.

"Robert wanted to fuck all of us: me, Kah-ren, his real sister, Nadia. Everyone except Verity. He tried, too. I had to fight him off a couple of times.

Nasty, pimply little twerp. He was at it again recently, too."

I was beginning to get a handle on it at long last. Sir Phillip Wilberforce and his wives had brewed up a deadly mixture. "What was special about Verity?"

"She hated Dad as much as Robert did. Robert hated his own father, too, but Verity loved hers like I—"

"I think he killed Nadia." I hadn't meant to articulate the thought, but it came out anyway.

"Jesus, no."

"You were going to say that you loved your father. Why did you shoot him?"

We were both up at the front of our stalls, near the gates, gripping the bars and staring out at the moonlit brick-paved yard. I moved sideways until I was separated from her only by the width of a brick wall.

"I'm insane," she whispered. "Paranoiac, depressive, schizophrenic. My life is a running stream of shit. I've tried—I've tried lots of things. I tried to talk to people. I tried. I wanted to be interested in them. Do you know why I had to leave Lindfield?"

"No."

"The council passed a law that you couldn't have more than one dog."

I didn't say anything, and she went on. "But I just couldn't . . . cope with things. I was interested in you, but you turned out to be another bastard. Just another bastard. Aiming your fucking gun at that poor dog. I went to see Dad to ask him to buy this place for me. I was so happy here. I could have got it going again, taken care of the dogs. Dogs are the only creatures—"

"Paula," I said, "your father hired me to find you. He loves you."

"He said no. He didn't understand. I had your gun, and I shot him." Her voice mounted into a scream of pain and rage. "I'd shoot you if I could. Oh, I'd shoot you, you murderer. You killed my beautiful dog. We would have been so happy here, Rudi and me. We *were* happy. He caught rabbits and—"

My patience gave way. I rattled the bars, trying to pull them from the mortar. Not a chance. I didn't want to die in a dog kennel. I cursed her and her father and every other member of her family. I yelled at her that they were all a pack of degenerates. She laughed and agreed.

"You killed my darling Rudi."

The blanket had slipped from my shoulders

during my outburst. I was cold and shivering; my skinned knuckles throbbed, and my bruised and bleeding head ached. Exhausted and drained, I sat down on the cold concrete. "He sprang at me like a fucking tiger," I said. "That big yellow bastard was a killer, and it was a matter of me or him."

"What did you say?"

"You heard me. I had to kill him. I didn't like doing it, but I had no choice."

"What did you call him?"

"A tiger, a yellow—"

Her voice, which had been harsh and off key, became soft, melodic. "Rudi's not yellow," she said. "He's a beautiful black and tan."

20

HER BOOTS SCUFFED THE CEMENT AS SHE moved close to her side of the pillar. I could hear her breathing and almost feel her warmth coming through the bricks.

"Not a smooth-haired dog, maybe part bull terrier?"

"Ugh, those ugly brutes. I gave up on them a long time ago. No, Rudi's a Doberman/German shepherd cross."

"Christ, those breeds don't take prisoners."

"He's fierce, but he's wonderful, and he's alive. I'm sorry I said—"

I was thinking fast. Crosbie couldn't be away much longer. "Does Robert know what Rudi looks like?"

"No, not unless he's been here since yesterday morning. Rudi's been missing since then. I've been frantic about it."

"Paula, for God's sake, whistle or call or whatever you do. We need him."

"What do you mean?"

"We need the dog. Robert's coming back to kill us. An attack dog might be of some help."

Her voice went cold again. "What are you saying? Robert's got a gun."

"He's got only one bullet—"

"You don't know that."

"It's probable."

"One's enough."

"I can't believe this. We're talking about a dog. We're human beings—"

"Yes," she said bitterly. "We are, and just think what we've been doing—what I've done, what Robert's done. We're wonderful, aren't we, we human beings? So kind, so loyal."

I could sense the madness rising in her again. "Okay, okay," I said quietly. "Think of it this way. We're all animals together. The lot of us. Particularly you and me in these cages. Animals fight for their survival."

"That's nonsense. That's—"

The sound of the Land Cruiser's engine stopped her. It approached fast, motor roaring, headlights blazing, and steam jetting from the exhaust. In the surge of hope I'd had I'd forgotten about the cold. Now it gripped me again, and I could feel my joints stiffening and my body cooling as if I were dead already. Crosbie pulled up with a showy skid on the bricks. He stopped a few yards from the cages with the lights full on us. There was something roped to the front. I squinted above the beams. It was the yellow dog. Its battered head hung loose and wet over the right mudguard.

Crosbie switched off the engine but left the lights on. He jumped down and pulled the pistol from his pocket. He slipped on the wet bricks, cursed, and strode away to turn off the hose.

Paula said, "Even a dog that ugly shouldn't have its head beaten in."

I didn't say anything. The point didn't interest me. I was going to die in a worse way than I had imagined, and I'd imagined some pretty bad ways.

Crosbie came back and stood in front of the cages. "Well, there he is, my dear little stepsister. Your precious Rudi. I always wondered about you and Rudi number one. Did you jerk him off or did you go all the way?"

Crosbie's laugh was drowned out by Paula's. She shrieked and howled and beat her feet on the floor. Crosbie took a step back. Then he yelled, "Shut up, you mad bitch!"

The lights were dazzling me, distorting everything. He was a dark, distant figure, twitching with agitation. I was a sitting duck. Even if I retreated to the rear of the cage, I'd be only three yards away from the gun and transfixed like a spotlighted rabbit. I stayed up there by the bars.

"Why did you kill Nadia?" I said.

Crosbie pointed the pistol at my head. "She was a slut, a whore."

Paula's voice was breathless after her fit of laughter. "And she wouldn't fuck you."

"Shut up! It was a sort of accident."

"Lamberte and Karen weren't an accident, though," I said. "How did you manage that?"

I didn't really care. I just wanted to keep him talking. While he talked, I drew breath. You don't talk to a dead man, not for long.

Crosbie took a clasp knife from his pocket and unfolded a long blade.

I watched, fascinated. *What the hell is he going to do with that?*

He seemed almost to be in a daze as he cut the ropes tying the big dog to the Land Cruiser. The body flopped onto the wet bricks. He put his foot against it and slid it across to the front of Paula's cage. "I found out about Karen and Patrick," he said dreamily. "I just couldn't stand it. Verity's the only person in the whole family who's got any goodness in her and look what was happening. Her husband and her sister . . ."

Paula chortled. "Who wouldn't fuck you, would she, Bobbykins? Didn't want your smelly little dick in her. Like me."

"That wasn't all I wanted," Crosbie said. "I wanted what we never had: love, warmth, understanding. Not those fucking boarding schools and tennis lessons and riding lessons and—"

"Poor little rich boy," Paula mocked.

"I tried to talk to Karen. I tried to tell her about Nadia. She said she'd go to the police if I didn't leave her alone. I *had* to kill her."

"How?" I said quickly. I wanted to anticipate Paula's next piece of derision, although I could see no hope in our situation. Crosbie was upset and shaky, but power is power, and a victim is a victim, unmistakably.

"She laughed at me. She told me she was going up to the mountains with Patrick and that she'd talk things over with him. They planned to blackmail me, and Paula was in it with them."

Paula spit at him through the bars. "You're wrong, Robert. But I did see Karen a few weeks ago. She told me you'd finally shown that you were as crazy as Nadia, as crazy as the rest of us."

Very deliberately Crosbie put two fingers of his free hand into the blood and brain tissue of the dead dog. The stuff was almost frozen, but his fingers came out wet. He daubed it on his face like a Comanche going into battle. He crouched, sprang to his left, brought the pistol up, and pointed it through the grille at Paula. I admit it; my first thought was, *If he shoots her, he can't shoot me.* But I screamed at him, trying to draw out the moment, the second, the instant.

"How did you do it, Robert? How?"

"I learned electronics at Sydney Technical College and explosives in the army reserves. I broke into Karen's flat and planted the device in her overnight bag. She kept it half packed with a transistor radio and a camera and stuff. It was easy. She told me when she was going. I calculated when she would arrive. It was easy."

"A clean sweep," I said. "After you kill Paula. Mind you, there's still Verity."

His head snapped around toward me. His deep-set eyes were small, dark points in his pale, smudged face. He looked like a badly made-up clown. The angle stopped me from seeing it, but indications were that he kept the .38 trained steadily on Paula's face.

"Not Verity," he said.

I was frozen to the bone, itchy and dying by inches, but Crosbie's agonies were sustaining me in a bizarre, unfathomable way. He dabbed more blood and gray goo on his face.

"Why not?" I said.

Paula's screech cut through with intensity and passion. "Because she does it with him. Don't you see? Little Bobby and Verity have been doing it since they were kids. Tell me, Bobby. Is she the only woman you've had? The only one? You'll never get another, will you? You can't kill her. Not Verity. Not your only love. Not your only cunt."

"Shut up! Shut up! Shut up! No! No! I would never. I couldn't . . ."

"Couldn't is right," Paula crowed. "Couldn't
—that's the problem, eh, Bobby?"

Crosbie seized the bars of the cage and tugged
on them. A ring on one of his fingers shrieked
against the metal. "I'll kill you," he shouted.
"I'll kill you now. Now!"

The big black and tan dog must have made its
leap from five yards away. It was nowhere in
sight, and then it was on top of Crosbie, throwing
him sprawling to the ground and tearing at him
with its paws and teeth. Crosbie screamed and
tried to seize its head, but the dog snapped at his
hands and kept digging its claws into his body.
Crosbie tried to roll away, but Rudi was too big,
too heavy, too motivated. He tore off an ear and
then sank his teeth deep into the flesh of Crosbie's neck. The man went limp. The dog
chewed on him a bit and then lifted its head.

"Rudi," Paula whispered. "Oh, Rudi." She
extended her hand through the bars. Confidence.

The dog eased itself up off Crosbie and padded across to Paula's cage. She made soothing
noises and fondled his ears and muzzle.

"Good boy, Rudi. There's a good boy."

I must have been holding my breath the whole
time. I let it out loudly, and the dog's head
turned in my direction. Its growl lifted the hairs

on my scalp and made me want to crawl to the back of the cage.

"No, Rudi. No, darling. It's all right, boy. He's a nice man."

The headlights blazed, the bricks were slick with Crosbie's blood. The dog I'd killed lay splayed out, one of its paws almost touching Crosbie's head. I shivered and felt my body weaken as if my blood were turning sour. The wind had lifted, and the cold was intense.

"Everything's all right now," Paula said.

"I hope you're talking to Rudi, not me," I said. "We're locked in bloody cages, and I'm freezing to death."

"I *was* talking to him, but everything *is* all right."

I could feel myself becoming unhinged. I laughed. "What the fuck do you mean?"

"You're in Rudi's kennel. I've got the key in my pocket."

"I don't believe it. You had the key all along? Why didn't you—"

"I thought you'd killed Rudi. Then you wanted him to attack a man with a gun."

There was no reasoning with her and no point. I put my hand through the bars nearest to the pillar. Rudi growled. I ignored him. "Give me the key."

Her pale, slender hand came through the bars, holding the piece of brass. I couldn't quite reach it. My fingers were stiff. She manipulated the key, trying to hold it out to the fullest extent. Rudi growled again, and I saw movement out of the corner of my eye. Crosbie was inching his hand across the bricks to where the .38 lay, glinting dully in the headlight beam.

"Another half inch. Come on!" I rammed my hand through the gap, ripping skin from the wrist. I still couldn't reach it. Paula saw Crosbie's intention and gasped. She dropped the key.

"Oh, my God. I'm sorry."

The little metal object was the most precious thing in the world, the most desirable, the most necessary. I pulled my lacerated hand free and shoved it under the bottom bar. My frozen fingers clawed at the bricks. I reached it, just. Got one finger across it, just, and flicked it back toward me. Crosbie's hand was inches from the gun. Sweat broke out on my face as I wangled the key into the lock, working awkwardly with three fingers. I got it in. I couldn't turn it.

Paula screamed. Crosbie had reached the gun. His face was a ghastly mask of blood and torn flesh. He slowly turned it toward us as he lifted the gun. Only his hand seemed to be capable of movement. His features were obliterated, but his eyes were bright and alive. He said something I couldn't understand. Blood gurgled in his throat, and he spit it out. Rudi made a tentative move toward him. Crosbie put the gun into his mouth and squeezed the trigger.

A spray of blood, bone, and tissue erupted from the man's head.

"Rudi, stay!" Paula said.

It took several minutes, but I finally managed to turn the key. The gate opened, and I crawled out onto the bricks. The air smelled of cordite and blood, but it was still wonderful. Rudi eyed me suspiciously, but I could live with that.

I looked at the woman crouched by the bars. Her face was chalk white, but she was smiling and murmuring to the dog. I went to the Land Cruiser and found a sweater and an oilskin coat. I pulled them on and discovered my half bottle of scotch in the pocket of the coat. And I'd thought some light-fingered cop had lifted it. I uncapped it, and the drink I took was one of the best drinks I'd ever had. Definitely worth another.

Her voice was steady. "What are you doing?"

"I'm drinking whiskey."

"Give me some."

I took a hammer from the tool chest. Rudi looked at me as I advanced with a hammer in one hand and a bottle in the other. I wouldn't have felt safe with an Uzi. He let me pass the bottle through the gate.

"Tell him everything's okay," I said. "I'm going to smash the lock."

"Rudi, stay!"

Rudi stayed. I broke the lock, and Paula came out. We stood together on the bloody bricks, and we both had a drink. Neither of us looked at Crosbie. The sweater, oilskin, and whiskey had warmed me. I was bleeding in about five different places, and fleas from Rudi's blanket had bitten me in five hundred, but I was beginning to think I'd survive.

"What now?" Paula said.

"I'm going to have to call the police. Is there somewhere we can wait?"

"There's a flat behind the kennels. No phone, though."

I went to the Land Cruiser, slipped the mobile phone from its cradle, and showed it to her. "The complete modern detective," I said.

21

IT WAS A LONG, COLD NIGHT, AND THE whiskey was a distant memory by the time we were finished. Police arrived from several different places and did a variety of things, including talking to Paula and me for hours. I tried to be patient. I didn't always succeed. Paula appeared indifferent, remote. She came to life only once, when someone suggested that Rudi be put down as dangerous. She spoke only three words to him, and the guy abandoned the idea.

Some of this took place at Fitzroy House,

some in the Mittagong Police Station. There were telephone calls to and from Sydney. In general, the cops weren't too unhappy with me. Two mysterious deaths had been explained, and they now had someone to charge over the shooting of Sir Phillip Wilberforce. They had a weapon, mine, to pop into a plastic bag and run tests on. This was once they'd prized it out of Robert Crosbie's dead hand. Not one of them suggested that anyone else had fired the last shot, although a pale-faced, long-nosed detective sergeant studied the hand long and hard and looked as if he'd like to make something of it.

Even dog lovers would have to be happy. They had one bad dog, dead, and one good dog, alive and a hero. Rudi ate a large tin of Pal out on the back step of the police station and looked around for more. Up close he wasn't that big, but he didn't need to be. He was all bone, muscle, and teeth. He commanded a good deal of respect, Rudi.

A woman who'd been a friend of the Wilberforces when Fitzroy House had been their holiday home was located, and she took Paula and Rudi in for what remained of the night. Paula would be taken to Sydney and charged, but there was no doubt that she'd be released on her own recognisances. Before she left, she turned to me and held out her hand. We shook formally.

"How is he?" she said.

I'd phoned Mrs. Darcy with the news. She'd reported that it had acted like a tonic on Phil. "Improving," I said.

"Good."

That was about as much concern for other people as I'd seen her express. Perhaps it was a good sign. Rudi padded away after her, and I was left with a couple of yawning cops, one of whom asked me if I'd like to sleep in a cell.

"No, thanks," I said. "I've tried that. The sheets are usually too rough."

"What sheets?" the wag said.

It was almost dawn by the time I got back on the road. I shivered until the heater took effect; then I sweated. I wasn't well. As I drove, I went through the whole thing in my mind again. It all fitted. Robert had recognized the background to Paula's photograph as Fitzroy House and made the connection. He'd got out here as quickly as he could to eliminate the other stepsister, whom he saw as a threat to him. All the questions were answered except the ones I'd started with: Who sent the box of bullets to Patrick Lamberte and why? I didn't know, and I decided I didn't care.

I turned off at Wombeyan Road and drove to Fitzroy House. All the coming and going had broken branches on the bushes growing beside the track and had flattened the grass growing up the center of it. A fine, bright day broke as I pulled up near the house. In the light it looked old and decrepit, but I could imagine Paula fixing it up and living there with a couple of dozen Rudis. I found my parka and the illegal gun in the wet grass. I was glad that I hadn't had to use the gun. Who was I kidding? I'd never had a chance of using it. I didn't visit the kennels. I had the feeling that I'd run my luck out there. If I went back, I was likely to slip on the bricks and break my leg.

I'd phoned Glen during the night, and she was up and waiting for me when I got to Petersham. She came out and met me on the bridgeway. She was freshly showered and wearing a black satin dressing gown. She looked like Ingrid Bergman in Paris in *Casablanca*. I felt like Bogie after he'd pulled the *African Queen* through the swamp. She kissed me anyway, risking blood, mud, whiskey breath, and stubble like a wire brush.

I put my arms around her, feeling her warmth, softness, and strength. "I'm sorry," I muttered into her hair. "I won't do it again."

"Yes, you will," she said, but she smiled.